Molly Giles' stories have always been among my favorites since I first read her work thirty-seven years ago. This collection is her best ever. What an irreverent original voice! I found myself gasping in shock and laughter, feeling at the end of each tale that I had garnered strange wisdom on the human heart and its unerring sense for finding trouble.

Amy Tan, author of *The Joy Luck Club*

The reader experiences an immediate immersion into the story and characters' lives . . . This partially comes about through masterful first lines.

Cris Mazza, 2020 Leapfrog Global Fiction Prize Judge, author of *How to Leave a Country*

With insightful prose and a sharp sense of humor, Molly Giles once again reminds us why she is one of the best short story writers writing today. Whether it is the tale of the beleaguered artist's wife angered by being overlooked or the quick sketch of two teenage girls offering a silent protest in the middle of a busy road, Giles' fantastic use of voice will have you clearly recognizing these characters and their frustrations. Smart and original, these stories capture the wild interior lives of people on the verge.

Luisa Smith, Buying Director, Book Passage Bookstore

MOLLY GILES

WIFE WITH KNIFE

STORIES THAT CUT

Leapfrog Press & TSB
New York and London

First published in paperback in the United States by Leapfrog Press, 2021
Leapfrog Press Inc.
P.O. Box 1293, Dunkirk, NY 14048
www.leapfrogpress.com

First published in the United Kingdom by TSB, 2021
TSB is an imprint of:
Can of Worms Enterprises Ltd
7 Peacock Yard, London SE17 3LH
www.canofworms.net

Cover design: Ifan Bates
Cover image © Jennifer Towhill, with thanks
Typesetting: Prepress Plus.

ISBN: 978-1-9485852-9-3 (US paperback)
ISBN: 978-1-9116731-8-7 (UK paperback)

9 8 7 6 5 4 3 2 1

Printed and bound in the United Kingdom

The Forest Stewardship Council® is an international non-governmental organisation that promotes environmentally appropriate, socially beneficial, and economically viable management of the world's forests. To learn more visit www.fsc.org

LEAPFROG GLOBAL FICTION PRIZE

Molly Giles's *Wife With Knife* was judged to be the winner of the 2020 Leapfrog Global Fiction Prize. Judge of the 2020 contest, Cris Mazza, said of Giles's entry:

The reader experiences an immediate immersion into the story and characters' lives . . . This partially comes about through masterful first lines.

Past Winners of the Leapfrog Global Fiction Prize

2020: *Amphibians* by Lara Tupper
2019: *Vanishing: Five Stories* by Cai Emmons
2018: *Why No Goodbye?* by Pamela L. Laskin
2017: *Trip Wire: Stories* by Sandra Hunter
2016: *The Quality of Mercy* by Katayoun Medhat
2015: *Report from a Burning Place* by George Looney
2015: *The Solace of Monsters* by Laurie Blauner
2014: *The Lonesome Trials of Johnny Riles* by Gregory Hill
2013: *Going Anywhere* by David Armstrong
2012: *Being Dead in South Carolina* by Jacob White
2012: *Lone Wolves* by John Smelcer
2011: *Dancing at the Gold Monkey* by Allen Learst
2010: *How to Stop Loving Someone* by Joan Connor
2010: *Riding on Duke's Train* by Mick Carlon
2009: *Billie Girl* by Vickie Weaver

These titles can be bought at: https://bookshop.org/shop/leapfrog

For Ralph

Acknowledgements

I owe big thanks to Cris Mazza, who chose this collection for the Leapfrog Press Global Fiction Prize. Tobias Steed and Rebecca Cuthbert at the Press have both been wonderful to work with.

My talented friends Rosaleen Bertolino, Audrey Ferber, DB Finnegan, and Marianne Rogoff have given invaluable feedback on many of these stories. Terese Svoboda and I have been trading work on a monthly basis for many years and I'd be lost without her. I've received support and inspiration from Tom Centolella, Kathy Evans, Toni Graham, Emily Kaitz, Janis Cooke Newman, Susan Trott, and Elaine Williams.

To all, my love and gratitude.

Table of Contents

Next Time

Her father hadn't said a word since Waterloo and Ginny, behind the wheel of the rented Renault, couldn't tell if he was asleep or angry, though why would he be angry? He had fussed about in the Wellington Museum for hours this morning and he had spent this entire afternoon stumping around the rundown Dunkirk seawall with an old military map in his hand while she trailed behind, pretending to be interested. He was doing exactly what he'd always wanted to do, touring the battlefields and war sites he had read about for years, and if she wished they were seeing more art museums and wandering through more outdoor markets, well, she could always come back to Europe later, couldn't she, on her own, after Papa was gone? She glanced over at him sitting erect in the passenger seat beside her, his brown collar pulled up, his brown cap pulled down, his sunglasses propped on his large nose, his swollen hands folded on the crook of his cane. He was almost ninety and would not last forever. "I love you, old terror," she said, knowing his hearing aid was turned off. Then she turned back to the road ahead of her.

Normandy looked as deceptively peaceful under the warm June sun as Belgium had. Fields of wheat and short green corn stretched on either side of the highway, interspersed with the black-hearted scarlet poppies they had seen everywhere. *In Flanders fields the poppies blow/between the crosses, row on row...* she had the rest written down in her journal to share with her middle-school students in the fall. She knew her father was seeing this placid countryside as the war zone it had been in the 1940s, all torn up, mud and barbed wire everywhere, helicopters landing and taking off, cots filled with the wounded and dying, but it made her too sad to think of it that way. The slaughter of all those boys? A waste.

"It had to be done," her father had stated calmly over dinner last night and Ginny had known better than to argue. Anyway, her argument was specious, for she had been thinking only of herself. One of those boys sacrificed in The Invasion, she'd been thinking, might have gone on to have a son and that son might have grown up to be the man for her, Virginia Jane Harris. If only her intended father-in-law had not been shot down in 1944, she reasoned, she might be sitting across from her soul mate right now instead of counting out pills for a cranky old man who still treated her as if she was fifteen. "It's bad Darwin," she decided. Her father had looked pointedly at the wine glass in her hand. "Hitler was bad Darwin," he'd said. This trip was hard on him too. Ginny had not been his first choice of companion. But he'd outlived everyone else, he'd been widowed twice, and his friends in the Rotary Club were dropping like flies. He was stuck with her, his only child. And it wasn't so bad. They were having fun. In a grim sort of way.

She eased the car now through the narrow main street of a postcard-pretty village lined with stone and half-timbered houses that looked as if they had stood there, untouched, for centuries, and glanced at the address she had written down.

Her father was paying for this trip, but he was a frugal man, and Ginny had not always been able to find inexpensive hotels with separate rooms for the two of them. More than once she had had to resort to Airbnb in secret. Her father would never approve if he thought they were taking advantage of the "new economy" as he called it, but Jean Luc's "Maison Musique" had sounded too perfect to pass up—private, secluded, close to enough ancient burial grounds to satisfy her father's hunger for history and only forty euros for the two of them. She had told Papa it was a B&B and he had accepted her lie without comment.

Following the scribbled instructions, Ginny turned into a lane lined with climbing yellow roses and tall pink hollyhocks. Leaving her father in the car, she parked behind an ancient Mercedes, slid out and went up to the front door of a white farmhouse and rapped. She could hear a television inside. There were dead leaves on the narrow steps and a pile of oily rags and automotive tools lay on the stoop. She began to wonder if her reservation had been clear—did Jean Luc know they were coming? She had not actually talked to him, just sent a text, in English. She rapped again, and when the door flew open, she stepped back so abruptly she almost lost her footing.

A man reached out and steadied her. Jean Luc was tall, about her age, strong and plump with cropped white hair and round blue eyes that brimmed with welcome. Ginny, never one to linger in matters of the heart, promptly fell in love, but regaining her balance was still able to say, "*Parlez vous anglais?*"

Jean Luc's grin as he shook his head No was so joyous that Ginny grinned back, barely able to stifle the deep silent laugh that had started to roll and echo inside her. This always happened when she met someone totally wrong for her, but it hadn't happened in years and she had almost given up. Still smiling, she explained that she did not speak French. "But my father..." she gestured toward the parked car. "He will be able to talk to you."

"You will not talk to me?"

"I will try."

"Yes? Inside, please. Wine? Yes?"

Ginny glanced behind her as Jean Luc drew her into the house; Papa might not be happy, but he was perfectly safe in the shade by the fence hung with roses. And the house seemed safe too, clean and modern, with a wall of bright family photographs. Nor was there anything to fear in Jean Luc himself. He was a clown. Barefoot, his large white legs in rumpled red shorts, he was walking backwards so he could continue to beam at her. What did he see? She was fifty-three years old for Gods' sake. She taught in an inner-city school and sang in a church choir. Her hair was badly dyed, her nose was peeling from yesterday's cemetery sunburn, her jeans were baggy and her breath stank. She beamed back.

"I see you like American music," she said, nodding toward the familiar face on his tee-shirt.

"You know Frank Zappa?" He clapped both hands over his heart. "I love Frank Zappa." He paused, his blue eyes troubled. "I do not," he offered, "like Neil Diamond."

"No one likes Neil Diamond."

"Oh. Ah. Ha ha. Thank you. You will sit?" He gestured toward a kitchen stool by the counter and patted his heart again.

"I should probably see the bedrooms first," Ginny reminded him.

"Of course. But first." He opened the refrigerator, empty except for a half dozen bottles of wine; he pulled one out, poured her a glass, and watched worriedly as she took a sip. The wine was too sweet, like Jean Luc himself, but she took another sip to assure him. Haltingly, as he settled, eyes luminous, on the stool opposite her, she began to ask him questions about himself.

She could not be sure of all the answers, but it seemed that he lived alone, had just recently started to rent out rooms, had left some sort of engineering job—trouble with a co-worker? a supervisor?—she couldn't tell. He played ping pong, did she know ping pong? He was a ping pong King Kong! Did she want to see his gold cups? No, of course not, why would she, they were not real gold, ha ha, more wine? Would she like to see what he kept in the closet over there? Look! Drums! A keyboard! Saxophones! And a guitar, yes, he played, no, not like Frank Zappa, maybe someday, but… "I show you, please?" He settled down on a hassock and played a ballad, which he sang to her, in French, blushing furiously all the while.

The familiar tap of the cane as her father came into the house made them both look up. The old man studied Jean Luc, who rose with a clatter and an outstretched hand. "Loopy de Loop," Ginny's father decided, under his breath, and then, turning to Ginny. "Drinking?"

"It's some sort of dessert wine is all," Ginny said.

Jean Luc continued holding out his hand and her father continued to ignore it. There followed a short exchange in French between the two of them, which sounded pleasant enough, Ginny thought, and then Jean Luc led them upstairs to the bedrooms. A not very clean bathroom with the toilet seat up occupied the first landing, and Ginny's heart sank, but another short flight led to two large airy rooms overlooking an orchard. Jean Luc moved to pull the door shut on a third room containing a rumpled futon and a computer desk overflowing with piles of laundry. "I do not expect you so soon," he apologized.

"Soon? We would have been here hours ago if my daughter hadn't braked for every wildflower. It's almost seven o'clock. We need to eat. Can you tell us where to go?" Ginny listened as her father asked again in French and Jean Luc answered gravely, looking so stricken that once again Ginny felt a giggle bubble up. "He says the only restaurant is miles away," Ginny's father translated. "And he wants to come with us."

"I will drive?" Jean Luc offered, leaning toward them, hands clasped, eager.

"Better you than she," Ginny's father agreed. "She's been drinking."

Jean Luc, looking from one to the other, asked, "Is all right?"

Ginny's father, stumping downstairs, said nothing but Ginny nodded.

"I will have bath first." He studied her face, worried. "You will not go away?"

"I won't go away." Ginny couldn't help it. She laughed out loud.

Still laughing, she followed her father down to the kitchen and sat beside him at a little table while he studied the map for their route tomorrow. They were going to drive to Paris, visit Napoleon's tomb, see the Museum of the Resistance and the Memorial to the Deported, all of which she knew were going to depress her deeply, and then they were going to fly to London to see the Churchill War Rooms, which, being underground, would be sure to depress her even more. She patted her father's shoulder, finished her wine, and went out to the car to bring their luggage in. She heard Jean Luc whistling from the bathroom upstairs and stooped to pet a black cat that lay curled under a trellis. Fat red hens clucked in the shade of an old barn and the apples in the orchard were almost ripe. She took a deep sniff of the yellow roses, wishing they were going to Giverny tomorrow instead of the Bastille but... next time. Her two favorite words. Next time she would go to Giverny with Jean Luc and they would marry in Ste. Chapelle and honeymoon on the Riviera. That's how time in France should be spent. She straightened, hoisted the two suitcases, and went back inside, pausing to study the photos on the wall. None of

Jean Luc with a woman. One brunette with red lipstick was attractive but looked too much like Jean Luc to be a wife—maybe a sister?

The restaurant that Jean Luc, freshly bathed and reeking of cologne, drove them to in his twenty-year-old Mercedes was a beer garden in a strip mall about fifteen miles away, crowded with young people and loud with canned music. Ginny's father took one look, turned his hearing aid off, ordered a steak and a coffee, and proceeded to eat. "He's a history buff," Ginny explained to Jean Luc, who listened intently but looked so troubled she was not sure what, if anything, he understood. "He loves war. No one knows why. He grew up in Quebec and none of his relatives were soldiers. He never served in any army. But when we moved to the States my mother toured the Revolutionary War sites with him, and later my stepmother went to all the Civil War battlefields, and now it's my turn. He's having a ball," she added unconvincingly, cutting into her salad and taking a sip of the amber-colored beer that Jean Luc had told her was brewed here. Both were delicious.

Jean Luc touched his pink lips with his napkin. "The war... for me, as a child, in Normandy?" Leaning forward to catch his meaning, Ginny seemed to understand that his family went to the beaches of Saint Laurent in the summer, where he and his cousins swam in craters made by Allied bombs. They collected shrapnel and shell casings and dove through the wrecks of war ships. "We find treasure," Jean Luc continued. "No gold. No jewels. But *crampons et moules*, we bring home to my aunt to prepare with butter and garlic." He patted his stomach. "Delicious."

"Children," Ginny's father scolded, looking at the two of them as they laughed. He asked Jean Luc something in French and Ginny saw Jean Luc's blue eyes become instantly somber. She finished her beer as the conversation went on and waited for her father to translate for her. "His great uncle," her father said, reaching for his cane, "was gassed in World War One and his grandfather was shell shocked in World War Two. So it wasn't all fun and games."

"No one said it was, Papa."

"Watch yourself."

Her father rose to go to the men's room and Ginny, chastised, waited until he was gone to meet Jean Luc's eyes. "My father wishes I was a more serious person. He actually thinks I'm a..." she began, then stopped, frustrated by her lack of French. Why had she never learned any language but Latin! Who could you speak to in Latin? Was "flibbertigibbet" even a word in Latin? Probably not! And why had her father decided, years ago, that she was one?

"He tells me you have many husbands," Jean Luc prompted.

"Yes." Ginny grimaced and held up three fingers. "No children. And you?"

Jean Luc fixed her with his blue eyes and moved his ringless hand back and forth across the tablecloth. "I have a special life," he said.

Ginny, warned (but of what?) sat back. When the check came her father paid it, overriding Jean Luc's protests. "Don't bother," her father told him, adding, unnecessarily and, Ginny hoped, incomprehensibly, "I always end up paying for my daughter's men."

Jean Luc's touch on her back as they went out into the parking lot was warm and light. She was quiet in the back seat as the two men talked, looking out at the dark fields. She had read in one of her father's books that over 16,000 civilians had been killed by bombs in this part of France before it was "liberated." All that death and mess and misery and for what? For her? So she could be an entitled peacetime princess bearing an old man's insults? What was he so bitter about? It was true her father had helped her out after her last divorce but she had paid him back. She had always paid him back. He just wanted to fight. Well tough. She wasn't a fighter. Never had been. The old man was going to have to deal with his bad temper and his bad manners on his own. No wonder he liked war! Tired, Ginny leaned her head against the seat and when Jean Luc glanced over his shoulder to smile at her, she smiled back.

In her room that night, listening to the frogs croak in the pond below her window, she wondered what she would do if Jean Luc were to appear in her doorway—but of course he would not. It would be up to her to go to him. She thought back to the walk she and Jean Luc had taken through the orchard after her father had gone to bed. Jean Luc had led her past the chicken coop and the barn to the old stables that he planned to turn into a concert hall. He had many friends, he'd told her, talented musicians, and people would come from all over Europe to hear them. Looking in at the abandoned animal stalls cluttered with tools, Ginny had said nothing. Every man she'd ever loved had had a dream as foolish as this. She could not believe she had come all the way to France only to meet someone so completely her type: lonely, naïve, hopeful, self-absorbed, and useless. Where did these men come from? And why did they always end up breaking her heart? She had turned to go back to the house and Jean Luc had followed, head down, but then, at the door, he had turned her around and kissed her. A clumsy kiss, half on her nose, half on her cheek, but sweet, so sweet she was still thrilled by it.

She slipped out of bed. Her father's bedroom light was out; he would be asleep by now, hearing aid off. Tiptoeing into the bathroom, she saw that the toilet seat was down, the floor mopped. Fresh towels were on the counter, and there was an opened bottle of bubble bath—Jean Luc used bubble bath!—on the rim of the tub. She giggled, peed, did the ritual stare in the mirror she always did before making a decision, turned toward her bedroom, rethought her decision, pulled a condom out of her purse, and went into Jean Luc's room.

It was like having sex with a puppy. Their lovemaking was quiet but surprisingly rowdy. Ginny was sniffed and snuffled and tickled and licked and patted and petted into a state of floating pleasure but returning to her own bed just before dawn, she was fairly certain she had not actually been penetrated. Not that it mattered. She felt replete. Content in a light floating afterglow. The beginnings of love were the ones she loved best, before the lover became depressed or needy or—like her last husband—abusive.

Her father roused her in the morning with a sharp knock on her bedroom door, and throwing on her clothes she met him at the foot of the stairs. He was packed and ready to leave. "Your boyfriend's still asleep," he said. "You must have worn him out last night."

"I don't know what you're talking about," Ginny said automatically, following him out to the car with the two suitcases. "And he's not my boyfriend."

"He's someone's," her father said, settling into the seat beside her and buckling up. "Did you see the photo of him on the wall? Red lipstick and a black wig. You sure do find them, Virginia Jane."

"Oh you know what, Papa? I forgot something. Just a sec." Going back into the house, Ginny bent to re-check the photo of the brunette on the wall—yes, that was Jean Luc all right, in drag, oh my. She reached for the guest book on the table, scrawled her email address on a blank page, brushed a tear off her cheek, and wrote "Next time." Then she went back to the car, got in beside her father, turned the key and backed out the lane to the street. She was halfway through the village when she looked in the rearview mirror and saw a barefoot man in red shorts chasing after them. Plump, breathless, the man held a spray of yellow roses in one hand and a basket of eggs in the other.

"Keep going," her father said, but she had already turned the motor off and unrolled her window as Jean Luc leaned in, panting. "For you," he said, handing her father the basket. "And for you," he said, giving Ginny the roses. Another damp, sweet, off-center kiss and he stepped back and waved.

After a few miles her father spoke. "What are we going to do with a dozen raw eggs?" he asked.

"I don't know, Papa. Food fight?"

Her father said nothing, but she saw him bite back a smile. Smiling herself, Ginny turned onto the freeway and headed for Paris, her lap filled with roses.

Agate Beach

"Amazing Grace" tinkles from hidden chimes as I push open the door to my sister's beach house. I haven't been here since the accident two years ago, and I wince as I step inside and pull back the thick, star-studded curtains to let in the light. Fairy rainbows flash from crystals, cherubs smirk from cheaply framed prints, gilded seraphim dangle and dance from the ceiling. Jackie has been collecting angels ever since Ryan died; it's her way of mourning, I guess, though what all these winged teddy bears and haloed puppy dogs have to do with my nephew, I don't know. Ryan was a great kid, but at sixteen he was far from angelic—a gamer, a shoplifter, and a stoner, he wouldn't have liked all these tchotchkes any more than I do, but he wouldn't have wanted to tear them all down and throw them in the dumpster either.

Jackie, always kind, blames my dark mood these days on midlife crisis, menopause, nicotine withdrawal, career burnout, and disappointment in love. When I told her I've been waking up in a cold sweat from nightmares at three every morning, she nodded and handed me a book from her grief group. "You're stuck," she said, "you've plateaued on the third stage. Anger," she added, helpfully, as I pushed the book back into her hand. "Go to the beach house. It's empty. Sort things out."

So here I be. I have broken off with my lover, left my husband, closed my dental office, cancelled my appointments, and driven six hours up the coast to do just that. I drop my duffle in the back bedroom, sweep the angel dolls off the angel pillows onto the rocking chair with the angel wings and go to the kitchen to find an angel glass for my bourbon. I carry it to the picture window to stare at the ocean. The ocean stares back.

Restless, I pull a bowl of polished agates toward me and begin to push the round ones to one side, the oval to another, but I can't get into "sorting" the way Jackie can, her French-manicured fingers rubbing over the surfaces like a mama cat licking kittens. Some of the stones are truly beautiful with their rich green, gray, and caramel colors, but there are so many of them! Jackie knows each agate individually and would miss any of the three million in this house if I were to pocket one, which I might, just to torture her.

I finish my bourbon. Dangerously tempted to drink the entire bottle—not, in my present state, a good idea—I head out to take a walk. It's afternoon still. The fog has burned off and the Pacific glints silver through the dark cypress trees. Following the old rutted road to the beach, I pass the trailer where the narcoleptic sleeps, the bright orange house that has been empty for years, the shell garden of the retired flamenco dancer.

The preacher who served time for embezzling church funds stops mowing his lawn; the stroke victim stares from her window; the young couple trying to live off the land look up from their marijuana plants. These are Jackie's friends. Jackie brings zucchini bread to their potlucks, organizes fundraisers to meet their medical and legal bills, sends birthday and get-well cards.

25

Agate Beach

None of them blame her for Ryan's death—why should they—and only I blame me. I pull the hood on my windbreaker up and raise my hand to mime good will as I pass.

Three of the houses on the left side have slid down the cliff in recent years and the end of the road has crumbled. The gray sand is firm enough to walk on with ease, though, and I head for the surf, which is high today. I pass a dead pelican, skull and bones stiffly feathered, fox prints still damp on the sand around it. Dead seagulls, dead sand crabs, dead jellyfish everywhere. Death death death.

On Ryan's grave, the words I suggested: *Too Soon.* Jackie has confided that when her time comes, Ryan will be waiting; he will take her hand and guide her through the pearly gates. His skin will have cleared up and his piercings will be gone. Being a dentist, I have to ask if he'll still wear his retainer. Jackie's eyes fill. His teeth will be perfect, she assures me. I turn to see his name carved on the yellow cliff behind me; I helped him carve it, years ago, both of us chiseling hard to make the letters nice and deep. Like me, Ryan thought his mother crawling across the beach on her hands and knees looking for agates was a hilarious sight, although unlike me he was willing to sit with her for hours after the agates were polished, helping her sift through the piles, both of them humming, content and off tune.

I see other names on the yellow cliffs as I walk—Kenny+Raylie, Liam+Gina. Where are you now, you crazy kids? Getting divorced, like me? Dating a man you met in a grief group, like Jackie? I pass a tumble of rust-colored rocks at the cliff base, a few plumbing fixtures from one of the fallen houses caught in the jumble, a garden daisy thriving in a damp crevice. I remember reading that a motorcyclist flew off a curve on the coast road last week. And what about that fisherman caught by the sneaker wave? And the child who disappeared from a campsite not far from here? Death, I think again. Death death death.

I walk for an hour and when I come to a driftwood log, I sit to do some of the "sorting" Jackie prescribed. The list is short. My husband asked if I'd been faithful and I told him the truth. My lover asked if I loved him and I told him the truth. I over-billed a patient and insisted on collection. I fired my hygienist even though she's Black. I yelled at a patient who wouldn't sit still. I rear-ended a lawyer in the parking lot of Trader Joe's. I told my neighbor that if he didn't shut his dog up, I would. I screamed at a recorded menu from Sprint. I left a restaurant without waiting for my meal, threw a lit cigarette out my car window, gave the finger to a cop, and returned a pair of jeans I'd already worn three times.

So sue me. I swear the only way to get along with anyone in this world is to fake it. Act nice, tell everyone what they want to hear and if they want to think that heaven exists or love lasts forever, shut up and let them. What can you do anyway? It's not like you can replace what you've lost and since what you've lost is irreplaceable, well, rack up your despair and depression and dismay and disgust to mid-life hormones, smack on an ex-tra nicotine patch, try another anti-depressant, eat more chard, walk another 10,000 steps a day, and tough it out. Pretty soon you'll be dead yourself anyway.

I yawn, watch a family of four search for agates on the shore-line—a young couple, their small child, a heavy-set woman in a floppy hat and long skirt who must be the grandma. All have shovels and are intent on digging. The old woman is a few yards behind the others, but she is the most determined. Trying to collect stones from the tide droppings, she stumbles down to the surf, digs intently, and stumbles back with each wave, shovel banging, skirt gathered up. I sift through the detritus of pale bleached shell and stone at my feet. Recently Jackie found a Coke bottle here, with a note in it. Some schoolboy had written his name and address inside for a prank and damn if Jackie didn't track him down and go see him and buy him presents and hound him until he stopped answering her calls. She mourns his loss; he was her consolation prize for Ryan, sent, she believes, by Ryan himself. Oh people.

I put my face down on my knees and take a deep breath and when I raise my head I see that the old lady is in trouble. She seems to be scrambling for something in the surf that is being drawn away by the tide, but she is in too deep, and when she loses her balance and falls, it looks like she can't get up. The others are walking ahead and don't see her or hear me when I holler to them. Well hell. I slowly rise, roll my sweat pants up, and stalk to the rescue. I hate having to do this. The cold current slaps against my calves and the sand shifts backwards underneath my feet as I reach for grandma, haul her up and pull her out. She is, surprisingly, as heavy as she looks. I set her down on dry sand, pat her shoulder, and trudge up the beach to alert her horrified family. Lots of thank yous, lots of bless yous. The old woman looks up with drenched eyes and presses something small and hard into my palm as I shake off the goodbyes and leave.

I'm shivering as I walk back to Jackie's—wet, cold, and edgily proud of myself. It's been a long time since I've done something good. I remember the retiree who had the heart attack under anesthesia; the little girl whose molar was fatally abscessed. I saved their lives too, I suppose. Of course I killed Ryan so these others don't count. Nothing counts. *Hey*, Ryan's voice on the cell phone, *Guess what, Aunt Sal, I've got the car. I know, no license, right, but you know Mom—yeah the way she goes no-no-no-okay-be-careful—and no I'm not high and hey why can't I talk and drive at the same time? it's no big deal hey don't hang up*—and the next minute my phone ringing and ringing and me

28

not answering it to teach him a lesson and Ryan bleeding to death in a country ditch, the truck that smashed into him never traced and how can *that* be sorted out?

It can't.

I push open Jackie's door, pinch my nostrils against the fresh assault of potpourri, strip out of my wet clothes, step into the shower, grasp an angel sponge in one hand, an angel bath gel in the other, raise my face to the spray. Am I going to be able to stay here all weekend? Can I bear it? Wouldn't it be better to drive back down the coast, find a bar and a cheap motel? Or better yet—drive further up the coast and just disappear?

Yes it would.

And no I won't.

It is not until the hot water's run out and I'm in one of Jackie's fluffy robes that I look at the thank you gift the old woman gave me—an agate, wouldn't you know it, in the shape of a heart. Or the shape she thought was a heart, which is of course wrong, as the actual heart looks more like a tongue than a valentine, and I have seen enough pulsing, beating, panting, bleating, lying tongues in my dental chair to know the difference. Still it must have meant a lot to the old lady for her to have scrambled after it into the surf like she did. Polished, it will be a dull unhealthy pink. I place it in the bowl with the others, towel my hair, and walk to the window. The sun is setting in B-movie glamour, ruby embers banked behind violet clouds shot through with lurid streaks of black and orange. The entire sky is in such brutal bad taste that I shield my eyes. This is the heaven that Jackie believes in? This painting on velvet is all Ryan was given?

No thanks.

I reach to close the curtains and a single ray of golden light suddenly shoots through the glass and gilds my bare arm. I raise it: a sword! When I swing my arm, it sparks. When I swing it again, a bright flame bursts out. Get back, death! Get back, grief! Get back, everything that is stupid and sad and just plain wrong in this world.

Tears fall down my face as my arm arcs and circles in blazing resistance, and until the light fades I lay everything low.

Protest

Two girls lie on their stomachs in the middle of the road, giving the finger to every car that passes. Most cars honk but a soccer mom stops, parks her SUV, and crosses over. "What are you doing?" she asks the girls. "Don't you know you could get killed?" Her cargo of little boys stares out the windows. The girls slowly rise to their elbows, eyes blank. Both are thirteen. Both are beautiful. "Fuck you," the dark-haired girl says. "Fuck you," her blonde friend echoes. A man in a pickup brakes. "What kind of language is that?" he shouts. "Fuck you," the girls say together, and put their heads back down on the asphalt. "You know what?" the man says. "You deserve to get run over." A grayhaired woman with an Earth First! sticker on her Honda leans out and calls, "Are they protesting? What are they protesting?" "They're protesting being teenagers," another woman says as she jogs by. "Drugs," an old man decides as he and his golf partner roll up the windows of their BMW. "Everything's drugs," the golf partner agrees. "Or worse." The girls roll over onto their backs, arch, stretch, look up at the sky. "Please get out of the road," the soccer mom pleads. The blonde raises her middle finger. The brunette does the same. The soccer mom walks back to her car, gets out her cell phone, and dials the police. "Don't ever grow up," she warns the little boys in the back. But it's already too late. She glances in the rear-view mirror and sees her own son's gaze slide away from her as he and his teammates sit silently, breath held, eyes shining.

Wife with Knife

Rafe was a drunk when I married him but he wasn't famous; fame came later, after his third one-man show. Suddenly everyone loved him. The students, of course—he'd been at the Academy for years so I was used to little girls phoning and fawning—but after *The Times* review it was society women and gallery owners and rock stars; my best friend Pamela was in there too, the snake, and I was sick of it. Every day when I came home from work there were new messages saying *O you're so wonderful/ come speak to our university/ come accept our prizes*. I should have been happy for Rafe but I wasn't. The man hadn't changed. He was still a miser, a bore, and a pessimist; he still had bad breath and athlete's foot and terrible table manners and I was still the frump chopping onions by the sink who got beat up twice a year. I guess I was jealous. So one night I stupidly reminded him that I too was an artist and had had my own one-woman show before I'd met him, and Rafe put down his glass and clenched his fists and I knew what was coming.

"Every painter's wife thinks they can paint" followed by "If you really wanted to paint, you would be painting every day" followed by "I couldn't stand to be married to another painter" followed by "I couldn't stand to be married to a bad painter" followed by "Which is what you are and always will be," and pretty soon he was going at me with the kitchen chairs and I was coming back at him with everything I could lay my hands on. While we were being treated in Emergency it occurred to me that I was as bad for Rafe as he was for me and I would do us both a favor if I would just get out. So I moved into a neighbor's barn with no electricity and no running water but it wasn't as bad as it sounds. A jazz guitarist moved in with me for a while and there were a few other men but nothing until the next year when I met Ashford Faught, the Scottish poet.

Ash wasn't as famous as Rafe and he didn't have Rafe's beauty, but he had one of those long faces, like a collie's, that I've always liked, and a virginal pink and white body, like a young girl's, and a marvelous voice, full of choked passion. He was very attentive, well educated, wonderful manners. He said, Come live with me, and I thought No, I can't do that, but when I heard Rafe had moved in with Pamela I packed my things and flew to Edinburgh.

Ash had a little cottage by the coast and we should have been happy there but we weren't. It was cold and gray by the water and we were cold and gray too, like characters out of a Bergman movie; the sex was good but everything we said was wrong. I had never lived with a poet before, and the silence was oppressive; I couldn't whistle or sing or dance to the radio when he was writing and the smell of turpentine gave Ash migraines so I could only work when he was gone.

He was gone a lot. He had two daughters in London and a young son in Glasgow and a mother in Dumfries. One Sunday he set off to see his mother and said he'd be back around nine. Nine came. Ten. Eleven. Twelve. At one, I decided to read his journals.

Wife with Knife

Ash's journals were these leather-bound jobbies with his initials in gold on the cover and inside they were "attended the symphony, enjoyed the Mahler especially," "just finished Keats's letters," all that crap, and the real life was recorded on little scraps of paper that were stuck in helter-skelter. I realized that Ashford Faught was a man who shook his journals out over a wastepaper basket on December 31st of every year so all that was left was this pristine record for his biographers to admire and be bored by.

Piecing the paper scraps together, I learned that Ash had been seeing three different women since he'd met me; two of them had fallen by the wayside but one remained and her name was Bettina. And you know, he'd even made a list with Bettina's name on one side and mine on the other and under Bettina he'd put "owns house in London" and under mine he'd put "was married to Rafe McAteer."

After I stopped screaming, I went straight to Ash's address book and found Bettina—it was four a.m. now—and I called and she answered and I said, "Hello, is Ashford Faught there, please," and she said, "Well yes, actually, he is," and I said, "May I speak to him, please?" and she said, "Just a minute," and then Ash came on and I said, "Hello Ash, it's me," and he said, "My god is anything wrong?" and I said, "No, nothing's wrong I just wondered when you were coming home," and he said, "I'll leave right now if you want," and I said, "Fine, if that will be convenient," and he said, "Actually it would be more convenient to come around eight tomorrow morning."

So we hung up and I went around figuring out ways to set his cottage on fire but instead I called Rafe and I said, "Honey, I just realized I'm once again in a place I don't want to be," and he said, "Then come back to me," and I said, "But you're with Pamela," and he said, "She doesn't need to know," and I said, "God you're a rat," and he said, "You like rats," and I had to agree. "I've started to paint again," I added but Rafe had dropped the phone by then and I could hear the Shostakovich he liked to listen to when he was working and I could imagine him standing in his studio with his bourbon in one hand and his paint brush in the other and I wondered if he was still painting those hideous portraits of me.

I sat by the door and when Ash crept in at eight the next morning, I asked him to choose, and he said he already had, he was just letting Bettina down easy because she was high strung and he didn't want to hurt her and why didn't we, the two of us, go off to The Highlands and be alone together. So we got in the car and drove up to The Highlands and it was awful there and I said, "You know, I really miss our walks on the beach, let's head back," and Ash said, "Right," so we headed back and we were in the cottage lying side by side on the bed when we heard a key in the lock and Bettina walked in. She looked at me and I looked at her and Ash threw his hands up and screamed something and ran out the door and out to the beach.

"What did he say?" I asked Bettina. "'I can't cope,'" she repeated. "Would you like a cup of tea?" I said. "What a good idea," she said.

We talked and it turned out Bettina and Ash had plans to get married. "I'm actually surprised you're even here," she said. She looked at me. "What was it like," she asked, "being married to Rafe McAteer? Weren't you his muse? All those portraits," she paused, "of you in the kitchen...?"

I was damned if I was going to respond to that, so I waited. She waited too. After a while she said, "Ash is deeply divided." Well in a situation like that someone has to win, and when Ash crept back in to beg my forgiveness, it looked like I was the winner, but another few days of me being quiet and him having migraines had us both so exhausted that I finally said, "Listen: why don't you go spend a week with Bettina and then decide," and he said, very quickly, "All right," and he got packed right away and I went to my friend Kiki's in London and she had this marvelous flat right by the South Kensington stop with huge windows and you could see the gardens and the guard horses and Kiki was in the theater there and soon I was meeting actors and musicians and dancers and after a week or two I began seeing Paul so I didn't go back to Ash again, nor did I ever go back to Rafe though I almost did once after he divorced Pamela, but by then he'd met the little waitress from Thailand and begun having those children he'd always said he didn't want, so it was too late. It hurts to think of the way he died, and I still argue with his ghost when I'm alone in my studio, furious that he wouldn't stop painting long enough to just go see a doctor and get the damn thing cut out.

Last week I went to his retrospective at the Met, like everyone else, and I stood there, like everyone else, while the docent stopped by his most famous painting and raved on and on about the color, the composition, the use of space and light. "Notice the abstract figuration of the woman chopping onions by the sink," she babbled. I waited for her to point out the almost imperceptible drop of red on the tip of the woman's knife. But the docent said nothing. No one ever has. The critics have missed it, the collectors have missed it, the biographers have missed it too. I'm beginning to think I'm the only person in the world who knows it's there, though for the life of me I'm still not sure if it's Rafe's blood or mine.

Bad Dog

Whiskery tub of muscle with flicks of spit and slime shot from spotted tongue and slick pink dick. Sly beggar eyes, wheedler's grin. The forelegs stiff in bossy supplication, the butt high, the propeller whirl of tail, the dance in place at the door, the stench of slept-in, spit-on hair and hide, the yellow sulfur farts, the bared teeth, the fetid breath, the slobber, the snuffle, the hurry up yip. Let him out! Let him in! Don't leave him here, secure in the house, warm in the car, safe in the yard! Take him with you! Let him dog you! Take the stick! Throw the stick! Take the stick again! Throw the stick again! Walk him! Not here! There! Not there! Unleash him, free him, see him circle, snarl, fight, bite, pee in six places, chase cars, attack strangers, spook horses, unseat cyclists, break the necks of sunning cats, gulp dead birds, roll in cow shit, chase squirrels up power lines, pack with Scout and Maggie and Bobo to bring down a fawn or a city child alone on the corner. Pick his dung up. Sack it. Schlep it. Pet him! Praise him! Feed him! Feed him horsemeat, cow-meat, chickenmeat, pigmeat, ratmeat, catmeat, zoomeat, road-kill, dogmeat! Gulp! Gone! Watch him gnaw the menstrual goo from your twelve-year-old's gym shorts, slop the snot off the baby's face, dig up the dahlias, bury the hiking shoe, chew the ankles of the antique bedpost, hump the limp leg of the Alzheimer patient, pull your guests' dinner off the dining room table, knock the vase down, flee as china and crystal crash to the tiles, plead guilty with hope-stricken eyes. Bad dog, good dog, come dog. Sit. Beg. Heel. Roll over. Down. Clown! you say. Comrade! Confidante! How cute he is! How clever, how comic. Look how he loves me! But how can he love you? He doesn't know you! He doesn't know you lied to your lover, stole from your mother, slapped your sister, abused your child, cheated your boss, falsified your taxes, perjured yourself in court, slashed your enemy's tires, slept with your best friend's spouse, betrayed your business partner, vandalized your neighbor, hit a pedestrian, slandered a co-worker—he does not know that you have behaved, all your life, in fact, like a dog—nor does he care. His interests are not your interests. His thoughts are not your thoughts. His dreams are of hunt, quarry, catch, and kill. His strange brain is at secret work in your house all night. Is it your house? Whose ghost startles your dog on the stair? Why does he bark at the mirror? What does he hear when the kitchen clock stills? Those claw marks high on the lintel of the locked door—where did those come from? And the flash of his moon-sharp teeth when you call? The grin of an exile, far from his kind, slavish, obedient, biding his time.

When in Roma

Dorte DeSwaart was the best scientist I ever hired: intelligent, inventive, industrious, disciplined, and persistent. A six-foot-tall beauty from Amsterdam, she had only been at Lamark Technology a year before she discovered the link to an important tumor-suppressive pathway that was going to win us a Nobel, at least. Aside from being our brightest hope, Dorte was also nice, just plain nice. I'd rush into the lab after catching a late shuttle from Palo Alto, sleepless after a long night spent wrestling with my two-year-old's tantrums, my six-year-old's insomnia, my ten-year-old's nightmares, and the six-month-old's asthma, my hair uncombed, boots untied, jacket splattered with baby spit, and there Dorte would be, handing me a cup of the hot cocoa she made herself, dabbing my jacket clean with spot remover, replacing the pot of dead ivy on my desk with the fresh roses she brought in from her own garden. Dorte was everything I longed to be: a calm, generous, sweet-tempered woman with a happy family, a successful career, and a brilliant future. "How does she do it?" I thought, splashing cold water on my face in the lavatory mirror after one particularly frazzled morning.

"It's easy for her," a harsh voice behind me said. "Her work is going well, she's about to make an important breakthrough, her husband hasn't moved out, and she doesn't have four children."

I looked up, startled. The only other person in the room was a small woman in a cafeteria worker's uniform.

"I didn't know I was talking out loud," I apologized. I waited. Had I been talking out loud? And even if I had—how had she known whom I was talking about? And how did she know so much about me? I turned to face her. A spy? The work we were doing at Lamark—Dorte's work with dysfunctional cilia especially—was delicate and needed to be kept secret. "Who are you?" I demanded.

The woman ignored me. "She'd give anything to have what you have," she said and turned to go. I was left with an impression of two gray eyes, heavily fringed with lashes, mocking me beneath a black baseball cap.

For the rest of the morning I thought about what I had heard, wondering if I had actually heard it. It was as if that odd little woman was excusing me, somehow, for failing to be as perfect as my research assistant, while in the next breath suggesting that Dorte, about to make "an important breakthrough," envied me. Envied me for what? My job? Ever since my recent promotion to Senior Director of the Oncology Department I had been under pressure—the job involved far too much administrative work—which I am not good at—and not enough time in the lab, which I love and used to—but who knew anymore—be good at. She wouldn't want my job and she surely would not want my marriage problems. Dorte's husband Fred was a gentle giant of a guy and their marriage, at least on the outside, looked solid. My marriage to Talc had always been shaky, nothing new there; we had survived the shut-downs of two of his start-ups and only his affair—if that's what it was— with one of his investors had kicked us over the edge. As for the children—did Dorte really want four children? My god. A faulty condom, a missed pill, a defective IUD, and, with the last, a drunken night of make-up sex with a sobbing husband in a gated, heavily guarded and hideous resort in Santo Domingo. Anyone could have four children under those circumstances. But maybe Dorte couldn't? I had heard her say she and Fred wanted children, lots of children, and that they hoped to have more soon.

They already had one. Lisbet was three, one of those impossibly beautiful little girls who don't look quite real. Dorte and Fred were both big-boned people with rosy cheeks, and though they'd left the Netherlands long ago they still looked slightly foreign in their handmade sweaters and clogs worn with socks. Dorte sometimes actually came to work in braids, and Fred, a medical technician at Stanford, wasn't embarrassed to be seen off duty at Peets in tie-dye. But Lisbet was tiny, elfin, with a dandelion explosion of red curls, a porcelain complexion, and a highly developed sense of style. On her laptop she'd point out Stella McCartney and Zulily designs, and her parents, sitting beside her, would eagerly order what she wanted. They adored her. Photos of Lisbet covered every free surface of Dorte's work station and she phoned or skyped or texted emojis to the child at least three times a day. On Friday afternoons she took Lisbet out of day care and brought her to work; we gave her a toy microscope to play with and she busied herself for hours drawing pictures of cells. She wanted to be a "science mama," too, she said, when she grew up.

One Friday, about a week after my encounter with the odd little cafeteria worker, Dorte brought Lisbet in as usual, but Lisbet was unusually whiny and restless and she soon tired of her coloring and her microscope and begged for gelato. When Dorte asked, I nodded yes, of course, they could leave and go get something to eat. Coming out of a meeting later that day, I was surprised to see them both still sitting in the cafeteria. Dorte's breaks rarely lasted more than ten minutes but here she was, at a corner table with, I was shocked to see, the same old witch in the baseball cap, who, hands waving, eyes flashing, seemed to be spinning some sort of fantasy which had Lisbet entranced, her gelato untouched. Dorte met my glance with a roll of her eyes. She had no use for storytelling, I knew that, because I had tried to give Lisbet a fairy tale book last Christmas at the DeSwaarts' annual cookie party and Dorte, politely, firmly, had placed it high on the mantle. "Don't you read to her at bedtime?" I had asked, surprised, and Fred, taking my elbow and leading me to the table laden with hand-painted plates piled high with fragrant *stroopwoffels* and *boterkoeks* and *Janhagels*, had said, "Yes. We read to her at night. But from ORIGIN OF THE SPECIES." I thought he was kidding, and laughed, but of course he was not; neither he nor Dorte made jokes and they never said anything that was not factual.

"What was that all about?" I asked Dorte when she brought Lisbet back to the lab for her backpack and jacket.

"Just a story," Dorte answered.

"About an egg," Lisbet said, excited. "This girl threw an eggshell into the ocean and it turned into a boat and she sailed away and was safe..."

"A story," Dorte repeated, patient. "Your friend came up and started talking to us..."

"My friend?"

"She said she knew you."

"No way," I began, but Lisbet interrupted.

"Can we come back for another story next week, Mama?"

Dorte smiled. "Of course *meissie*. If you want to."

But Lisbet didn't come back the next week. I don't know exactly how it happened; my own week was taken up with administrative meetings, organizing the upcoming international conference in Rome, fights with Talc and endless schedulings and re-schedulings of soccer practices, swim practices, day care cancellations, PTA meetings, doctor appointments, lawyer appointments, and physical therapy sessions with the baby; I did try to emulate Dorte and say "If you want to" to my family and assistants once or twice and I did of course notice that Dorte was absent from work but I didn't get the whole story until Fred emailed to tell me that Lisbet had died.

How? Dorte volunteered nothing but I had found in working with her that if I asked direct questions she would answer directly and that is how, over the next few months, I slowly found out the details. It seemed that after they went home that Friday night Lisbet developed several large open sores on her lips and inside her mouth. Their pediatrician told them this was not uncommon. He said that her fever would break soon and the sores would clear up by themselves. He advised them not to take Lisbet to the hospital. Lisbet wasn't in any pain, though she looked like she should be; she was sweet and quiet as ever, singing that depressing nursery rhyme "Ring Around the Rosie"—the same song the baby liked so much—and drawing eggshell boats. She was completely recovered by Tuesday but then, overnight, bam, open sores again. Dorte and Fred panicked, overruled their pediatrician, and took her straight to Emergency. That was Wednesday. By Thursday Lisbet was dead. She had picked up a renegade staph infection in the hospital which had torpedoed straight through her tiny body—those open sores were an open invitation for infection and none of the doctors could save her.

A lot of couples can't survive that sort of tragedy. Talc and I, who couldn't survive even an evening together at that point, would have been destroyed if anything happened to any of our children, but Fred and Dorte never blamed each other—or the doctors—or the hospital. They just grieved. It was hard to watch. They didn't have a funeral—they were agnostics—and after a week, Dorte came back to work. She walked around as if she was made of broken glass, but she monitored her zebrafish with her usual attentiveness and she was as calm and caring as ever, the one who took your eyeglasses off and cleaned them with a soft cloth, the one who brought you hot tea and spiced cocoa, who asked about you and did not speak about herself. The kids and I would see her and Fred silently riding their bikes through the Stanford campus or out at Crystal Springs Reservoir on the weekends, cheeks flushed, legs steadily pumping, and they always greeted us with a friendly wave, but the evenings of Indonesian take-out and ping pong in their cottage stopped and we were not surprised when they politely refused to accept the season tickets to concerts at the Montalvo Arts Center that Talc and I did not have the heart to go to together.

No one saw them socially until Dorte, to my relief, hosted her cookie party months later on December 5th. Coming in with the children, the baby in my arms, I was shocked to see Lisbet's trike still on the front porch, her water wings still on a patio chair by the pool and her big wicker chest of dolls and stuffed animals still open in the living room. My three oldest filled their plates and went into the game room immediately to watch videos, but the baby wanted the toy box and I saw it was safe to set Happy down beside it, for the glass coffee table, its edges still padded with bumper strips, was cleared of books, vases, and knickknacks, and when I carried my gift bottle of brandy into the kitchen I saw sippy cups and a Peter Rabbit china set in the cupboard and Cheerio boxes and juice pouches stacked on the pantry shelves.

"It's like they can't move on," I said to our marriage counselor, when I told her about it the next day.

"Really?" she said. "It sounds to me like they *are* moving on. They're probably saving these things in hopes of having another child soon."

"Maybe." I was hesitant. "They're already in their forties."

"That's not too late," the marriage counselor chided. "The important thing is to keep on trying." She looked first at Talc, then at me. "Don't you agree?"

We did. Talc and I had been "trying" as best we could and around the beginning of that next year he finally moved back in. It wasn't easy for us to be together—his irritating little he-he of a laugh, my careless cracks—and we weren't patient people, like the DeSwaarts, but at least his girlfriend had gone back to Korea, I had stopped my raging jags, and the children had calmed down. When it came to the kids, we both agreed on one thing: they came first—and agreeing on that helped us agree on other things.

We had been lucky with our children. They were a rowdy group, high strung and highly accomplished. Our oldest, Harry, had just scored in the 99th percentile on his Sixth Grade SAT, Hilary captained her soccer team, swim team, and gymnastics team, Hannah played a flawless violin solo at a recent New Mozart recital, and Happy—well, we just wanted Happy to live up to his name, and so far he had. I tried—and failed—not to brag about them, and I also tried, and failed, to ignore Dorte's hungry looks at the Facebook photos I used as screensavers. Now that I understood she and Fred were trying to get pregnant I saw all the signs—the way Dorte bolted from the lab at odd hours to meet Fred at home, her uncharacteristically dainty walk down the corridors when she returned, her countless doctor appointments, her pallor and the dark circles under her eyes. Despite her obvious exhaustion, her work had never been better. Her recent discovery of a previously unknown function of the p53 gene had us all excited. But Dorte, always conscientious, refused to reveal any of her findings until she was sure they were correct. I nagged, but it got me nowhere. Despite pointing out that her discoveries could, once published, not only win us every major prize in the world but lead to the actual cure of pancreatic cancer, Dorte could not be pushed.

One evening when we were both working late, I brought my tea over and sat down beside her in the cafeteria. Scientists are night owls and neither of us was tired, though we agreed we would not mind owning a few helpful robots—I wanted one to dictate letters and departmental memos and Dorte said she'd like one to help Fred in the garden. "So much of what is coming out in technology today still seems like magic to me," I admitted.

"Magic?" Dorte shook her head. "There is no such thing as 'magic.' Only common sense, applied sensibly."

"Galileo was an astronomer who believed in astrology," I reminded her. "Newton was an alchemist who spent his life trying to turn lead into gold."

Dorte wagged her finger at me, unsmiling. "You're teasing," she said.

"What about all these new inventions at the fertility clinics? Have you and Fred had any..." I almost said *luck*, but stopped myself, "positive results yet?"

"No," Dorte admitted, dropping her eyes. "We have not tried everything yet of course, but we have tried clomiphene, metformin, ICSI, IUI, so many IVFs..." her voice trailed off. "Six IVFs. None of them took. It surprises me," she said, frankly. "Before I met Fred I was pregnant all the time."

"Miscarriages?" I asked.

She gave me a puzzled look and I looked away. Who knows why I never even considered abortion for myself. Surely I should have when the amnio results came back on Happy. But I hadn't. Talc hadn't. On that, we'd been united. Or crazy. Or arrogant.

Thinking we were super powers who could handle the special demands of a Down Syndrome baby and still be good to each other and to our other children.

"I'm sorry," I said. "Maybe, next week, at the International Conference? Why don't you bring Fred to Italy this year? Sometimes just getting away helps. And Rome is so..."

"Rome?

The harsh voice was familiar and we both looked up. Before we could say anything, the cafeteria crone, whom I had not seen in months, pulled out a chair and sat down. She had a feral smell that despite myself I half liked. But she paid no attention to me. Her gray eyes were on Dorte.

"I have a friend in Rome who can help you," she said. "A fertility doctor?" Dorte asked politely.

"A Roma."

Dorte looked at me.

"Gypsy," I explained, and raised my eyebrows. Dorte was the last person in the world to go to a fortune teller.

"Miracle worker," the woman corrected me.

"Dorte and Fred don't believe in miracles," I said, smiling, but Dorte, reminding me I had a meeting, blew me a kiss, waved me away, and turned toward the old woman. My cell buzzed; I had to get back; I left them there.

I love Rome; Talc and I honeymooned there, years ago, but I was almost glad he decided to stay home with the children this time; I was overwhelmed with the thousand niggling tasks needed to make the conference run smoothly and for the first two days I scarcely left the hotel. On the last afternoon I finished my duties early and escaped from the stuffy conference rooms without being noticed; I had a few hours to wander through the Jewish Quarter, buy a few presents, peer over the bridge into the Tiber, and just sit with an espresso at a cafe in Trastevere before I had to get back.

When in Roma

It was while I was returning through the piazza by the ancient church of Santa Maria that I saw a blonde head, crowned with braids, gliding high above a crowd of Japanese tourists. "Dorte!" I called. I hadn't seen either her or Fred since we'd arrived; hoping they'd been holed up in their room making a baby, I hadn't even resented Dorte's last-minute decision not to present her findings on the p53 gene. Calling her name again, I pushed through the crowd but she was no longer by the fountain where I thought I had seen her. Turning, I saw her climbing the church steps with a young girl. The girl could not have been more than fourteen, a slim teen with tangled black hair, and, when she turned to glance behind her, I saw she had a silver ring in her nose and the same astonishing light gray eyes I had seen on the cafeteria worker. A beggar? Dorte was notoriously generous; I had seen her give ten-, even twenty-dollar bills to the homeless asking for handouts at the Sunday farmers market. But Rome wasn't safe little Palo Alto. Remembering reading in my guide book that "any able-bodied beggar is probably a robber," I decided to follow them.

It was dark inside the church after the glare of the piazza and it took a second for my eyes to adjust. Except for a few scarfed women kneeling in front, the church was empty.

Puzzled, my eyes passed over the domed golden ceiling with its rich mosaic figures to scan again the vacant pews. No one. I shrugged. Dorte in a church? Not likely. She must have slipped out a side exit the minute she saw where she had been taken. For some reason, however, I lingered. I found myself standing by the door and though all I did was stand there, I felt something bubble up, not a prayer exactly, but an exhalation, a little breath of gratitude. I had so much. I closed my eyes. Thinking of my children's faces, Talc's tentative smile, the work I was permitted to do in the field that I loved, *Thank you*, I said. Thank you.

When in Roma

The farewell dinner that night was lavish, twenty courses at a restaurant by the river, and in between the artichokes and the lobsters and the pastas and salads and the toasts and bad jokes and grandiose plans for the next conference, I glanced across the table to Dorte and Fred. They were sitting shoulder to shoulder, eating everything on their plates, chatting with their neighbors. I was not surprised to see that Dorte was the first to notice that the elderly doctor from Hungary was choking and to perform a swift efficient Heimlich's that saved his life, nor was I surprised to see her take the elbow of a young clinician from Detroit who had had too much wine and help her off our bus and back into our hotel. There was no chance to talk to her alone that evening or on the flight back to SFO and it wasn't until a few weeks later that I was able to again sit beside her in the cafeteria with my tea. "So," I said, joking, "did you see the Roma?"

"Yes."

"You did?"

"Yes."

"And did she," I chuckled, "work 'miracles'?"

"Yes."

"You're pregnant?"

"Yes."

"How?"

"The usual way," Dorte said drily.

"No. I mean—a spell, an amulet, a..." I paused. "What exactly did she ask you and Fred to do?"

"We ate the grass off Lisbet's grave."

I was silent.

"We sucked the raw meat out of seven snake eggs."

"Dorte."

"It worked," Dorte said, her voice fierce, and pushing back her chair she stood up and left me.

That night, in bed, I told the story to Talc. He asked a question that had not occurred to me. A businessman's question. "What did it cost?" he asked. "Cost?"

"What kind of deal did they strike?"

"I don't know. They must have given her a lot of money. Or maybe," I joked, "Dorte traded her soul."

"Soul," Talc repeated. His voice was flat. But the way he said it sounded a lot to me like *Seoul*. The next morning I went downstairs while he was still asleep and went over the leather upholstery of his car with a piece of scotch tape. Sure enough. A single hair, long and black, caught in the driver's seat headrest. His "investor." His rich, young, beautiful "investor." Back from Korea. He had probably been with Jin-Joo the entire time I was in Rome.

This time Talc left the house without apology and I sent him off without tears. But we were all devastated. Harry's grades went down, Hilary's teams lost every game, Heather threw her violin against a wall and broke it and even Happy, sensing what was going on, lost his appetite and had to be coaxed to eat. Dorte no longer met me with a cup of hot cocoa, and, as her belly grew, her experiments became uncharacteristically sloppy; she seemed to have lost interest in even her beloved zebrafish. One morning as I drove in I heard a news flash on the radio— Italian scientists had discovered a property of the p53 gene that could cure pancreatic cancer.

I confronted her in the lavatory. "You gave that gypsy girl all your research findings," I said.

"She wasn't a gypsy," Dorte muttered.

"Roma," I corrected but then, seeing something dark and strange twist Dorte's face, I blurted, "Was she a spy?"

Dorte didn't answer. "You traded us in for a baby." I waited. "Didn't you?"

"Yes."

"You're fired."

She left without protest that day but seeing her empty work station and looking at the great mess of memos and emails and requests clogging my computer screen gave me an idea. I went to the head of Lamark Technology and asked to be demoted. I was given Dorte's job which, thanks to Talc's alimony, I could afford to take. I have loved it ever since. I have always been happiest with a pipette in my mouth. I am a good solid hardworking research scientist. I have always believed that just because a phenomenon can be explained one way doesn't mean it can't be explained in another. The world is still a mystery to those of us trying to understand it. As for Dorte's defection? For some reason it hasn't bothered me as much as it should. Italian scientists will be taking home the Nobel Prize and that's all right; I am simply glad that her findings made it out to the public, and that people all over the world are standing a better chance of being cured now as a result, and if that isn't "magic" I don't know what is.

After I heard that Dorte and Fred had had a son, sold their cottage, and moved to Italy, I did do a little reading on the Roma, not much. According to one legend, they are strays on earth because they refused to shelter the Virgin and her child in their flight to Egypt. According to another legend, they are capable of sending souls safely to Paradise on eggshell boats. I hoped that was the story the cafeteria crone had told Lisbet, perhaps to comfort her, and I would have asked the old woman, but I never saw her again and no one I spoke to had any memory of her at all.

I didn't see Dorte again either, not for years. Then one Sunday, buying produce at the farmers market downtown, I felt Happy tug my hand. He was twelve then, not quite five feet tall, droll and dimpled, with a five-thousand-word vocabulary and a good sense of humor. He led me to an open trailer selling bakery goods—the same array of *stroopwoffels* and *boterkoek*s and *Janhagels* that I remembered fondly from the December cookie parties. Looking up, I saw Dorte carrying a fresh tray to the table.

Her hair had grayed, she had put on a great deal of weight, but her cheeks were still rosy and her hazel eyes were still direct and frank. She pressed my hand warmly and invited Happy and me into her trailer to meet her children. She had four now, she said. We entered gingerly, for the trailer was strewn with toys and pieces of clothing and felt dark, cramped, and dirty. Fred, bald and gaunt, rose from the shabby couch where he had been watching television and proudly introduced us to their oldest, a sullen ten-year-old boy who, for no reason, pinched Happy, trying to make him cry (Happy doesn't cry) and to the two tall blonde cross-eyed sisters wrestling on the floor. He offered to let me hold the three-month-old baby, which I did, for a minute, before handing it back.

"He has teeth," Happy whispered.

"I know," I whispered back.

We both shivered, took the plate of cookies Dorte pressed on us, and made our way back through the market. Passing a table piled with cheap plastic crucifixes, horseshoes, crystals, and rabbits' feet on key chains, Happy stopped. He pointed to a jumble of evil eye pendants and looked up at me with the pleading expression I have always found it hard to refuse. Happy wants so little. The old man behind the table lifted two of the blue glass amulets and swung them back and forth hypnotically. "Magic," he said.

I started to explain that we didn't believe in magic, but one look at the old man's light gray eyes stopped me and I reached in my wallet and bought both of them.

The Sowder Sisters

Ruby was fine until she gassed herself. I must of told her a hundred times, "If you don't keep that stove lit, Sister, you're going to blow yourself sky high." But oh no, ninety-four years old, stubborn as sin, never once paid me the simple courtesy of listening to a single word I said and this despite the fact that I graduated Branch Normal and know a thing or two—and what did Ruby do?—but work all her life for the telephone company. So what did I smell when I came by her house last time but gas and after I covered my mouth and nose with a tea towel and opened all the windows and turned the stove off, what did I see but Ruby, sitting straight up on the commode, naked as a jaybird, biggety as you please, scolding a Black man, a fat lady, and a little boy—three people only she could see. "Go long now," she was telling them, "You don't belong here!" and she was still shooing them off even after 9-1-1 came and took her away. Turned out the gas didn't hurt her lungs none, Ruby's healthy as a horse, nothing wrong with her body, it's her mind. So now she lives with me. She don't like the cats and that's all right, I can keep the cats in the cellar, but keeping Ruby inside is another matter entirely and lately I've had to tie her to the bed.

Mostly she just lies there but sometimes she talks. Once she said, "Why you got that big black spider in your hair?" and even though I knew there was no big black spider in my hair, I about dropped her supper tray and Ruby winked at me and smirked like she used to do. Yesterday she pointed at the ceiling and said, "Why you got rain raining inside your house?" and when I looked up to see if the roof leaked, she laughed. Ruby has a real mean laugh. She's seven years older than me, made me wash the Packard every Saturday but never once let me drive it, kissed Ned Nichols at my picnic dinner, always said she asked for a monkey but got a sister instead. So tonight when she asked me to take the gum out of my mouth and give her half, I said No. "Even if I had any gum in my mouth," I told her, "which I do not, I would not give you so much as a taste," and I was about to slam out and leave her when Ruby laughed again, only this time her laugh wasn't mean, it was scared, and I sat down beside her and held her hand and we sat in the dark like that for a long long time.

Accident

On my way to the airport I hit a Christian. This was in Siloam Springs, Arkansas, on a hot afternoon last August, and it was entirely my fault: I wasn't looking. I'd stopped at a red light and had just punched the CD player off because Levon Helm was making me miss Jed and I was sick to death of missing Jed. When the light changed, I started up. The white pickup in front of me did not.

Cursing, I pulled over to the shoulder. As I reached into the glove compartment to get my insurance forms, I heard a rap on the window and saw a red-faced man glaring at me through the glass. When I opened the door, he leaned in, grasped my hand, hard, and dropped to his knees on the gravel.

"Let us pray," he said. It was not a request. He pressed my hand so firmly to his chest I could feel his heart thump against my palm. "Dear Lord," he began, "Guide thy errant daughter that she may receive the gift of the Holy Spirit and be washed in the blood of the lamb. In Jesus's name, Amen."

"Thank you," I said, pulling my hand back.

"Amen," he corrected. He glared at the tattoo on my ankle, two bluebirds that were supposed to be Jed and me forever. His eyes moved over the spill of cigarettes and make-up the impact had scattered across the front seat and, as I tried to tug my skirt down, lingered on an opened package of condoms lying on the floor.

"I'm awfully sorry," I said. "I hope you're not hurt." The man closed his eyes and rose to his feet. He was about sixty, in work boots and overalls. He didn't look hurt. He looked strong and he looked furious.

"Get your cell phone, Sister."

"I don't have one. Don't you?"

His lips moved silently.

"I thought I was the only person in the world without a cell phone," I said.

"Get out."

Shakily, I got out and looked at his bumper. It wasn't bad. One small dent next to the fish decal. Then I looked at my VW. The license plate was smashed and the right headlight dangled like a plucked eye. "Jesus Christ," I whistled. I felt my hand grabbed again.

"Lord," I heard, a hiss of tight rage, "remind me that this blasphemer is Thy beloved child." When he opened his eyes to look directly at me, I was alarmed by their blueness. "Let's go," he said. And before I could even get my purse, he led me by the wrist down a gravel embankment into a strip mall. His walk was stiff and rapid. Helpless, I trotted beside him as we passed an IGA, a gun store, a pawnshop and a Dollar Tree. The asphalt around us sparkled in the sun and small American flags, strung at regular intervals along the shops, hung limp in the heat. We finally stopped at a low brick storefront at the end of the complex. A sign over the door said *Glorious Grace Fellowship*.

A large blonde sat at a reception counter under another sign that read *Rejoice*. She took one look at us and rose. "Pastor Mike!" she said. "What happened?"

Accident

"Accident," Pastor Mike said. He pointed at me.

"Do you want me to call the police?" the blonde said.

"Yes," Pastor Mike said. "I surely do." The blonde picked up a white phone, dialed, and handed the phone to the Pastor. "I'll let Miss Edna know you'll be late for supper," she said.

Supper? I looked at my watch. It was three o'clock in the afternoon. My best friend's plane was due to land in Tulsa at six. We were going to celebrate my break-up from Jed with tequila martinis and float the White River tomorrow. I hadn't been to the river since the time Jed and I had seen a baptism, a preacher dunking an entire family, mother, father, and seven skinny children, in the shallows. I'd wanted to stop the canoe and take pictures but Jed wouldn't let me. It's not done, he'd said. It's not done here. Trying not to worry about what was done here when you broke the law, I picked up a magazine lying on a nearby table, glanced at the cover, which showed a baby wrapped in tissue with a gift card saying "From God" and was about to read a recipe for Coca-Cola cake when I felt a familiar grip on my wrist. "Sister?" Pastor Mike said. "Let's go."

I followed him back to the street. The police were already by our cars, a stout woman officer with a ponytail and a stout male officer with no hair at all. Their uniforms looked heavy in the heat. They knew Pastor Mike, he knew them, the blonde followed us out and they knew her too. The woman officer shook her head when she saw the front of my VW. "How'd it happen hon?" she asked, the compassion in her voice making me tremble as I admitted, "I wasn't looking." I handed her my papers and she turned to the others.

"California," she announced.

"No wonder," Pastor Mike said.

All four turned to stare at me and I thought of California with a pang: its rundown freeways teeming with Atheists, Buddhists, Confucians, Druids, Gnostics, Hari Krishnas, Hindus,

Jews, Muslims, Rastafarians, Scientologists, Shintos, Sikhs, Taoists, Wiccans. If I rear-ended anyone in California, I might be sued or shot but I would not be prayed upon. How had I ended up so far from home? It was because of Jed and his redneck charms of course, but why had I fallen for Jed in the first place, or, having fallen, followed him here, or, having followed him, stayed? Why had I thrown away my good iPhone just because his voice was on it? Why had I put his Levon Helm in the CD player instead of my own Otis Redding?

I blinked back tears as the police officers radioed their dispatcher. "Y'all all right?" a voice called from a passing truck, and as Pastor Mike waved, another car pulled onto the shoulder and dislodged three women who, hurrying forward to embrace her, could have been the large blonde's sisters. A car full of teenage boys pulled over to comment on Pastor Mike's bumper, and an old man struggling up the embankment from the strip mall took it upon himself to start fixing my headlight. An earnest little girl appeared out of nowhere with a box of powdered donuts which she passed around. No one was paying any attention to me. A butterfly hovered over the brown-eyed susans blooming on the roadside; a mockingbird called from a flagpole; the air smelled of honeysuckle and fast food and diesel. I had almost forgotten why I was there and was startled when the police officers turned back to me.

"Next time, look where you're going," they said, returning my papers.

So I was not going to be cited? I hesitated, unsure, until the bald officer turned to a man in a Razorbacks tee-shirt and asked about deer season and the female officer put her arm around the little girl with the donuts. Thrilled, I said, "Thank you!" and backed away to my car. Just before I turned the key I looked in the rearview mirror and saw Pastor Mike's blue eyes burning into mine; I hesitated, but when I lifted my hand to

Church News

Liz Valdez and her five children always sat in the same pew—the first one to the right of the altar. Since Liz has been excommunicated, so to speak, that pew has remained empty; sometimes newcomers to St. Stephen's Episcopal don't know any better and sit down there and then Lamond or one of the acolytes has to take them aside at Coffee Hour and explain that it upsets the rest of us to see that pew occupied. *Oh,* one visitor from Memphis said, without, as far as we could tell, any sarcasm at all, *is that space sacred?* and Lamond almost choked, you could see him getting red above his surplice and *Nonono,* he said, *it's not sacred, it's just...* (poor Lamond, he should never have been chosen to replace young Father Dressler) *it's just special.*

Liz Valdez *was* special, no argument there. Not beautiful but, as Dr. Wolcott said, no one ever looked at her just once. Something about her made you stare. Not tall, not thin, not well dressed in her raggedy hemmed dresses, but there was some serious fire in those brown eyes and her lips looked, and I say this as a happily widowed eighty-year-old woman, delicious, a plump red candy heart stuck right underneath an unremarkable nose and above an already falling-down chin. None of us ever

61

saw a Mr. Valdez and he may not have existed. None of Liz's kids looked Latino, in fact they could have been a litter of mongrel pups, all shapes and colors. Little Otto, well, he was a Black boy, but his sister Madelyn was a redhead, the twins were practically albinos, and Paulie, the youngest, I swear Paulie was Asian. Four different fathers and none of them a Valdez is my guess but I never had the nerve to ask Liz and no one else did either.

Bill probably did, Bill Collier, the now-ex-choir master; when Bill was still with us he was pretty outspoken. Liz was painting houses when she first came to town and Bill's wife Merlee hired her to do the front porch, God knows why, pity probably, Merlee always had a soft heart for strays. So Merlee goes merrily on teaching Fifth Grade at Harrison even though Bill's at home with a back injury practicing his organ, excuse me, and next thing you know Bill is announcing he's fallen in love for the first time in his life; he posts Liz's face all over Facebook, hires Rick Cordova, the crop duster, to skywrite her name over the mall, and no one is surprised when he buys a triple-wide and Liz, Otto, Madelyn, Paulie and the twins move in with him, leaving poor Merlee stuck with a porch that needs at least two more coats of Sunny Day Yellow before she can even walk on it.

Soon there's a wedding and Liz wears, are you ready? White. Bill is all tender and nervous, the kids are dressed like little dolls, Merlee is weeping in back of the church, the choir is nervous and off key, the rest of us are sort of confused but the ceremony is right here at St. Stephen's and we wouldn't miss it for the world. Young Father Dressler, Bill's best friend, says it's a miracle that two such sad and lonely people have found each other and his blessing is full of heart and soul, though he has to raise his voice over Merlee's sobs.

Time passes. Liz never misses a Eucharist and though she's busy painting houses all over the county with a team of teens that Stan the Youth Leader cobbled together for her, she still finds time for the Monday yoga and Thursday meditation classes and twice a week she helps out in the kitchen with the community meals. Bill's back is still too bad for him to conduct the choir, so Stan steps in and we don't have to wait long for the next act. There's Stan's fiancée in the Wal-Mart buying nine rounds of ammunition, there's Stan in a new leather jacket tooling around on a Honda motorcycle with Liz in back, there's Bill hitting the Main Street bars. Pretty soon Bill and Liz are going to couples counseling with young Father Dressler, pretty soon Stan is going to couples counseling with them, pretty soon Bill stops going, pretty soon Stan stops going—pretty soon Liz keeps going—and keeps going. Every. Single. Day. Mrs. Manis at the parish desk isn't nosy exactly but she did tell us young Father Dressler's office door stayed locked during those sessions and that the only sounds she could hear, not that she was listening, were not the sounds of two people praying.

Young Father Dressler, poor dope, comes clean to the congregation soon after; all shy and pitiful he announces his feelings for Liz, and asks her to stand up in the front row. She does, hair a rat's nest like always, faded sundress of some sort, and the little dog pack rises with her. Father Dressler asks us to accept Liz as his intended though he has to raise his voice to be heard over Merlee's laughter. Stan was long gone at that point; he'd left his fiancée and gone up to Oklahoma City, and after the divorce Bill disappeared too, someone said he'd found a job with a church in Missoula, someone else said he'd moved down to the Delta and started to work on a fishing boat though how he could do that with his bad back, the poor guy could barely move, none of us could figure out.

Another wedding, this time at city hall, because Mrs. Manis petitioned against having it here in the sanctuary. Soon after the ceremony, Father Dressler's sermons began to take a serious turn toward the dark; he no longer inveighed the Holy Spirit or enthused about the Sacred Dance of Love but started sounding like a Baptist, ranting about the Devil and the dangers of lust, and then, three months later, the police get a phone call, a man's voice whispering that there would be a dead body by the lake in ten minutes because he's about to shoot himself and to please come get the corpse before some hiker stumbles over it, so Jimmy Doherty and Cal Perron race out there, sirens blaring, but too late, young Father Dressler is curled at the foot of the biggest oak tree looking, Cal said later, like a little boy taking a nap.

No note, no reason, and although Dr. Wolcott has suggested there may have been some funny business on Father Dressler's computer—child porn is Dr. Wolcott's guess—the mystery remains unsolved. Liz kept coming to St. Stephen's as if nothing had happened and that's when Lamond had to tell her she had to go. He told her the parishioners didn't want to see her which isn't really true, we're more or less fascinated by her. I think the truth is he doesn't trust himself to see her kneeling before him at the communion rail with those candy-colored lips pooched out and those dark eyes firing crotch shots. Liz didn't protest, she was about through with this town anyway, and she and her kids go to St. Jude's United in Harrison now and from all I've heard they are doing fine. There are always rumors of course and I suppose it's possible she could be pregnant with Dr. Wolcott's baby or she could have won that scholarship to divinity school, but the only rumor I believe is that she and Merlee are now an item. Mrs. Manis heard that the new African rector at St. Jude's plans to hold a commitment ceremony for them soon, and when she told us that we all clasped hands and bent our heads and prayed, not for Liz or for Merlee, we have faith in them, but for that poor young man from Nairobi who has no idea what he's in for.

Deluded

On her seventy-fourth birthday my friend Viv woke late and lay in bed for an hour, then phoned to tell me she was cutting her step kids out of her will, firing her therapist, and turning her housekeeper in to immigration. She had a lump in her right side that was probably a burst appendix and a ringing in her left ear that felt like a brain tumor. She might as well kill herself, she said, what was the use, no one cared, just get it over with, make everyone happy, right?

She waited.

Then: "Right???"

After I said I couldn't agree more and suggested she gas herself in the Lexus instead of drowning herself in the hot tub, she hung up on me, took two Ativan and rose at last to shuffle into the kitchen. Her kitchen was cool and dark and huge and empty. Expensive new appliances stood unplugged against the wall and the counter housed an array of dead orchids and empty bird cages. She made herself tea on a hot plate and was, she told me later, gnawing a leftover chicken leg when she remembered she was supposed to meet yet another contractor at noon. Tough, she'd thought, picking a bone splinter out of her dentures. He was probably a crook like all the others she'd fired and she was damned if she'd make herself decent for him, but when she glimpsed Scott Campbell's golden head and broad shoulders gliding up the path toward her front door she ducked back into her bedroom, threw off her old flannel nightie, struggled into yoga pants and a cashmere sweater, clapped on a wig, and applied a quick slash of lipstick. She didn't have time to put on shoes and answered the bell in her bare feet and bunion pads.

Scott did not seem to notice. "He looked straight into my eyes," Viv told me at our Thai place the next week. "And it was electric."

"He was that shocked?"

"You laugh." Viv glared at me through her trifocals and reached for the rice. She had already told me that Scott Campbell was "a bit younger"—forty-four—and I had already whistled at the thirty-year age difference, which Viv, chewing as always with her mouth open, had ignored.

"Something deep passed between us, Nan. Very deep. I'm thinking I may have found The One."

"The one contractor you're going to keep, you mean?"

"No, Smarty. The ONE. Scott is the most intelligent person I've ever met. Not book smart like you maybe, but people smart. You know?" She fixed me with a hard stare. "He's very intuitive. He got me right away. And I got him. Hey. What time is it?" She thrust her wrist with the Cartier watch she can't read under my fork.

"Late."

"I've got to go." She reached for her shawl and rose. "I have to stop at the bank before it closes. Scott likes to be paid in cash."

"I bet he does," I began but Viv was already out the door. The check for our lunch, I saw, lay unpaid on the restaurant table and I reached for it with a groan. I too was a widow in my seventies, but unlike Viv, I wasn't a millionaire.

I thought about Scott as I laid down the tip. Viv had been married and divorced twice in the thirty years I'd known her and in between husbands she'd had countless affairs, mostly with her doctors and then with the lawyers she'd hired to sue her doctors. None of her relationships had lasted long and all had ended badly. She was no longer the beauty she once was; her hair had thinned, her face had fallen, she wore two hearing aids and panty liners. Why was she so eager to court another disaster?

Scott did not seem to mind being courted. Tall and sunburned, he stood pleasantly smiling when Viv finally introduced us. He didn't flinch when she laid her cheek against his shoulder and hugged him, though he did not, to his credit, hug her back, and when he showed me the work he'd done on her kitchen I almost liked the guy. He'd repaired the skylight, knocked out a wall to let the garden in, refinished the wooden floor, and laid handsome new granite on the counters. It was a stunning transformation. Viv didn't cook but if she did, I said, this would be the place to have a dinner party.

"A party?" Viv repeated, her voice dreamy. She turned at once to Scott and cooed, "Will you come if I do?"

"Wouldn't miss it," Scott said.

Scott didn't miss much. He suggested that all three bathrooms could use remodeling, that the living room could be extended and that Viv's bedroom suite should have French doors and a balcony. To everything he suggested, Viv said "yes."

Now "yes" was not a word Viv used lightly. She took meds for depression, anxiety, insomnia, OCD, and panic attacks; she slept with a stuffed monkey she'd had since she was six, argued loudly with librarians, waiters, policemen and salesclerks, cut everyone off in traffic, talked incessantly and exclusively about herself, returned items after wearing them for weeks, kicked my old dog Maverick every time she came over, and got us disqualified from our last women's doubles when she threw her racquet at a referee—no one knew why I'd put up with her so long and I didn't either. All my other friends had dropped Viv long ago. My book group told her they were disbanding and then began meeting in secret; my bridge club found excuses not to include her, my tennis partners shuddered when her name came up. But for some reason I'd always admired Viv—her energy, her fire, her stubborn drive—and I'd stuck it out.

"You like difficult people," my late husband once said.

"That's not a compliment," I'd guessed.

"No," he agreed, turning to go back to his workshop, "Just an observation."

Observing Viv after Scott came into her life, I began to see a few changes for the better.

Viv started to behave. She paid her housekeepers, pool people, and gardeners on time, dropped a few lawsuits, forgave the loan to her stepdaughter, and stopped phoning me with complaints every morning. It was a good deal all around, I thought, good for Scott, who was making money hand over fist, and good for me, freed from the thankless job of trying to cheer Viv up every morning. I was tired of reminding her that she had the health, wealth, and opportunity to do anything she wanted.

"But all I want," she said simply, at one of our lunches, "is to be with Scott. You don't understand because you're content with your little life. But I still feel things. I'm adventurous. Passionate. Scott sees that in me. He knows that about me." She paused, dreamy. "We have so much in common, Scott and I. Alcoholic mothers, distant fathers, all sorts of abandonment issues. We both," she finished, "had unhappy childhoods."

"First or second?" I snapped, stung. My life wasn't "little." I had two grown sons and was expecting my first grandbaby in six months. My husband had not been easy to live with but I had mostly happy memories of our long marriage; I wasn't interested in seeking another. I had a million friends, both men and women; I did volunteer work at the literacy center and the thrift shop; I knit and read and gardened; I had Maverick. "Look, Viv," I said, keeping my voice even, "isn't all this in your head? I mean, really—tell me the truth: has Scott even asked you out yet?"

"Asked me out?"

"Dinner. Movies." I paused, unable to imagine it. "Dancing."

"No. But I have kissed him."

"How?"

"What do you mean how? I just reached up and grabbed him."

"Did he kiss you back?"

"No. But he said it was nice."

"Nice," I repeated, hoping she heard that. Nice: dull, safe, non-sexual. I shook my head and caught our reflections in the restaurant mirror. I saw myself: a plump old broad with gray hair, complete with wrinkles, pouches, jowls, my tits in my lap, my lap covered with dog hairs. Viv should have looked just as bad, but somehow she didn't. Her cheeks were flushed, her eyes sparkled, so maybe, I thought, Scott Campbell actually was attracted to her, miracles happened, lots of women had younger lovers. But just then Viv shrilled for the waitress and sent her spring rolls back, refusing to pay for the rest of her lunch, and I thought, No.

It wasn't until the remodel was finished and Scott was about to start work for someone else that Viv decided to buy a condo across town. It needed to be completely rebuilt, she insisted, and Scott was the only person who could do it. The few times I glimpsed him that summer the man seemed on tiptoe, half out the door, calm, smiling, uncatchable. But he *was* caught, Viv explained. He was in love with her. No he had not said so. No they had not had a meal yet. No they had not seen a movie or gone away for a weekend; they had not kissed again; they had not had sex. He was waiting for the right time, she explained. He wanted everything to be perfect. "You all right with that?" Viv barked. "Or do you want to argue more?"

"I'm not arguing. I'm..." I stopped. I didn't know what I was doing. Despairing. Had Viv lost her mind? I smiled at the waitress who had hesitated in the doorway when Viv's voice started to rise. "I just don't want to see you get hurt."

"I'm not the one who is going to get hurt," Viv assured me. She leaned forward. "Do you know what Scott's dream is?" she asked. "He wants to build a greenhouse—one run on solar, with all organic materials and a sod roof. And I," she said, sitting up and throwing her napkin down, "am going to give him that!"

"Won't that cost a fortune?"

"I have a fortune," she reminded me. "We're looking at some property tomorrow. I've ordered a picnic. And a bottle of wine."

Viv dressed for the picnic in harem pants, a low-cut silk shirt that hid her hips, and Italian sandals; not surprisingly, she wrenched her ankle trekking after Scott through the fields, but it was worth it, she told me later, because it meant that Scott had to pick her up and carry her back to his truck in his "big strong arms." She was bedridden for the next two days and had to leave the rest of the search to Scott, who immediately found five acres nearby and soon, surprise, Viv had bought the farm.

It was none of my business. I knew that. Still, when I envisioned Viv's future, I saw that as soon as the "greenhouse" was finished she'd probably buy a sailboat (Scott loved to sail), or a resort in the mountains (Scott loved to ski) or a hacienda in Mexico (Scott spoke Spanish!). Clearly Viv had never heard the phrase "cash cow" and I was not about to spell it out for her. She had always done exactly what she wanted to do and if she was willing to buy a man who was willing to be bought, well, good luck to both.

The next few weeks were busy ones for me. I had promised my husband to find a home for his collection of antique weapons after he died, so I spent my days on the computer, looking for a dealer willing to take them. The Library and Literacy Center was having a fundraiser and I had to help the Chair with publicity on that, and poor Maverick's Addison's Disease had kicked in again, requiring numerous trips to the vets for treatment.

Things were not going well for Viv or Scott either. Scott had hurt his back carrying Viv across the fields that day and work on the greenhouse was slowing down because Viv, regressing to her previous habits, had fired the architect and neglected to sign the permits Scott needed, which required multiple "conferences," as she called them, in her bedroom as her ankle healed. I ran into Scott walking back to his truck after one of these conferences, one hand on the small of his back, his eyes downcast. "Hey," he said, bending to pet Maverick's head. "Can you talk to Mrs. Blackstone for me? You're her friend, right? The thing is," he gave me a half-hearted smile and shifted his weight like a boy, "she hasn't been writing the checks lately."

"You have to beg?" I guessed.

"I can't pay my men."

"He'll get his money," Viv said later, when I told her. Her ankle had healed but she had begun to use a cane, which she tapped on the restaurant floor to get the waitress's attention. "He'll just have to earn it."

"Whoa. I don't like the sound of that."

"Cover your ears then. Scott's gone now anyway. He had to see his sick father up the coast somewhere. He'll be gone for two weeks. I offered to go with him but he decided it's best I keep an eye on things down here. He hated having to leave me, but… Hey. Where are you going?" she asked as, weary, I set down my half of the bill and rose from the table.

"It's Thursday. I go to the farmers market downtown on Thursday."

"Whatever for?"

"I like the music."

"What kind of music?"

"Blue grass."

"Scott likes blue grass. Wait a minute! I'll come with you."

The farmers market was more crowded than usual and I let Viv off at the entrance while I searched for a parking place. I was in no hurry to join her and paused to buy a few pounds of the last Gravensteins of the season and a basket of the first persimmons. As I wove through the colorful booths I looked up and suddenly saw Scott. I should not have been surprised, but I was. He looked so ordinary, just a young blonde guy in cowboy boots and a work shirt standing with his arms around a dark-haired girl near the music stand. They were swaying back and forth to the fiddle when an old woman in a black shawl pushed through the crowd and whacked him on the back with a cane.

"Jesus!" Scott screamed, turning around.

Viv hit him again, this time in the chest. She was raising her cane to hit him a third time but a bystander grabbed her wrist so she kicked him instead. I watched Scott double over and I felt rather than heard a little snap, like a scissor snap, cutting any tie I had ever had to Viv clean off. I was through. It had taken thirty years but I was done. I turned, made my way through the crowd, and drove away.

Viv never asked why I abandoned her there; she didn't seem to notice that I had. She drove up to my house the next afternoon and hobbled toward me in her house slippers as I knelt in my garden, planting bulbs. She said that I'd be interested to know that she and Scott had made a deal. After he agreed not to press charges, she agreed to let him continue work on the greenhouse. With one condition. He must apologize.

I looked up at that. "Apologize?"

"Honestly, Nan," Viv said, "talking to you is like talking to a four-year-old. Scott cheated on me," she explained. "And if he wants to be paid he has to stop seeing that cheap little hair-dresser or whatever she is and promise not to step out on me again."

I set down my trowel and got to my feet. "He calls you Mrs. Blackstone," I said.

But Viv had already driven off. That evening I fed Maverick and watched my shows and went to bed. But I couldn't sleep. After two hours I turned on the light and sat up. I saw my "little" life as Viv must see it: my stacks of library books, my shapeless bra and panties thrown across the bars of the exercise bike, my jeans tossed on the floor by my Birkenstocks, the vase of autumn roses on the bureau, petals falling, and there, at the far end of the bed, my old dog, with his white muzzle and bleary eyes, dead asleep. I got out of bed to cut another Ambien into fourths when I heard an owl call outside. I slipped through the front door and stood shivering in my nightgown in the driveway. The moon was old and lumpy but it still shed light everywhere. I bent to retrieve my trowel, glinting silver in the dirt where I'd dropped it, and suddenly thought of spring, when all the bulbs I'd planted today would be in full bloom, and I'd have a new grandbaby to hold and Maverick, god willing, would still be padding around, and I lifted my face to the sky, overwhelmed by its mystery.

Assumption

Mary had had it. The kids—kids?—Seth was forty and Stefani was forty-one—had been fighting since San Cristobal. *You are I am not Yes you are.* Cramped in the back seat of the tiny rental car, Mary translated their back-and-forth invectives into Spanish for the softness, the quick prettiness of the language, but her pulse beat with impatience and her stomach churned and curdled. "Would you two knock it off?" she said at last. "This is supposed to be a fun trip."

"Mother," Stefani warned. Mary shrugged and turned her hearing aid off. Seth had a large gray mole on the back of his neck that trembled when he shouted, and Stefani already had deep frown lines. They had been a beautiful couple when they first married but they were a haggard, adulterous, materialistic twosome now. It was not her fault. Not her business.

Fucking spendthrift—Mary read Seth's lips as he turned in profile, mole bobbing, and Stefani, equally unimaginative, spat back, *Fucking miser.*

If we did nothing else right, Mary thought, Stefani's father and I knew how to fight. She tried to find a comfortable place among the garden urns, serapes, sombreros, wrought iron wine racks, woven rugs, and hammocks that jammed the back seat. Several extremely sharp-edged tin mirrors reflected her face upside down, doubling her double chin and the bags under her eyes. She smiled anyway, remembering the handsome old boatman who had given her a wink as he oared them through a lake strangled with floating lilies at the resort.

She turned to the window. The mountains in this part of Chiapas were a soft hazy blue. The air outside, she thought wistfully, probably smelled of wood smoke from dinner fires, small good dinners of roasted corn and chicken marinated in limes and chilies—she'd never know, because Stefani insisted on windows up, a/c on. Speeding, Seth swung around stocky Mayan women in embroidered blouses walking single file along the edge of the forest, dark-faced men bicycling back to their villages. Every now and then a few shacks appeared. Mary waved to the children standing in their dusty yards with their dogs, but they didn't wave back—why should they?—just another old American lady, passing by.

Her stomach gave a decisive lurch. "I'll need a bathroom soon." She could never tell how loud her voice was with her Telex off; not very loud apparently, because neither turned to acknowledge her, though Seth, scowling, waved toward the scenery as if to say: No gas stations, no towns, no bathrooms. The road curved and wound, around and around, into the clouds. Mary rubbed her belly and sat back. She had always loved car trips; she was a good traveler. San Cristobal had been her favorite city so far, and its cathedral, where, kneeling, she had celebrated the Feast of the Assumption that morning with beautiful brown-skinned women in brocaded blouses, men in pink serapes, teenaged soldiers, and a vanload of chatty French tourists, had been her favorite place. But some fruit she had bought from one of the shawled vendors on the cathedral stairs was not setting right. She could feel an evil fluid begin to burble and bounce inside her. "I'm getting sick," she announced.

I told you not to eat those plantains. This was Stefani, mouthing. *They were fried in pig fat but oh no, you had to have them.*

"They were delicious," Mary explained. Stefani grimaced and sat back, and Mary, her hand pressed to her abdomen, grimaced too. The plantains had not been delicious. They had been green and greasy and she had only eaten them to spite her know-it-all daughter who had eaten nothing but protein bars since Merida. She had been an idiot to bring Stefani and Seth to Mexico. Just because she had had the happiest years of her childhood here—years ago—did not mean that they would enjoy what she enjoyed: the soft warmth of the mountain sunshine, the earth colors of the sky at dawn. She smiled, remembering the lively community of expatriate artists her parents had reared her in. She'd had a childhood of flowers and fountains and fiestas, and she would trade it for nothing. She snapped her hearing aid back on and leaned forward, hoping to distract the kids with stories of her happy early life but a new stomach cramp stopped her.

She pursed her lips and pressed her buttocks together, trying to suppress an insistent fart, but it exploded anyway, and she watched as Seth and Stefani turned to accuse each other and then, in a helpless rush of shame, she felt her bowels loosen altogether and flood her jeans. Horrified, she tipped her head back and closed her eyes.

"She's dead!" Stefani cried.

Oh honestly.

Still, it was a good idea. Mary kept her eyes closed.

"The smell!" Seth swerved so that one of the mirrors tipped and scratched Mary's arm. "I can't take the smell."

"My mother's dead and all you can think about is the smell?"

"I don't like the smell of dead people, okay? Is that okay with you? It has nothing to do with your mother, per se."

"Per se? Excuse me? This is my mother we are talking about!"

"Well what do you want me to do? What are we going to do? Tell me what to do."

"We have to find a hospital."

"How?"

"I don't know! We need to find some Mexican and ask for help."

"We don't speak Spanish. Only your mother speaks Spanish."

"Only my mother *spoke* Spanish."

Brakes. Seth throwing up by the side of the road, Stefani outside screaming at him. Mary opened her eyes. It was dark. She was surprised. She wasn't aware that much time had passed. Maybe she really was dead. But no. She could smell herself. It wasn't that bad. Just natural human shit. It didn't feel that bad either, cooling around her ass and thighs like a mud bath in a spa. Still, it was humiliating. As old age was humiliating. As being in the back seat with children in charge was humiliating.

"I can't drive with her in the car," she heard Seth say.

"We are not going to leave my mother, who paid for this trip in the first place, if you will recall, dead by the side of the road."

"I was thinking," Seth, humble, low, "we could strap her to the top of the car."

"Do what?"

"Strap her on top. Until we get to a phone."

Silence.

"Until we find a hospital."

Silence.

"It's the only way I'll be able to drive, honey."

Mary opened her mouth to protest but nothing came out. Stunned, she made herself stiff as the corpse she was supposed to be, as, nagging and gagging, the two people she had once loved more than anyone in the world wrapped her in a rug, hoisted her up, and strapped her to the roof with rope from one of the hammocks. When they got back inside the car and began to drive she opened her eyes and stared up at the stars. She could smell the smoke now and the deep smell of the pines and feel the cold fresh wind. She had never felt so free, so lonely, so invisible or so angry. Below, she knew her daughter and son-in-law would still be fighting. They had fought over the house she had bought them, the dental work she had paid for, the debts she had settled. They didn't mind fighting. They liked it. They probably even liked each other.

I'm the one they don't like, Mary thought. I'm just an inconvenient old lady with a convenient bank account. She began to cry, then let herself once again be taken by the beauty of the night sky above her, and eventually, despite the irregular jolt of the car beneath her, she fell asleep.

When the car braked, she awoke. Struggling up, she saw they had stopped before a dusty little outpost sitting all by itself at the edge of the forest, lit up like Christmas with green and red bulbs. She heard the kids dash out of the car and run toward it. She would wait until they returned and then she would confess and tell them the truth and they could all fly home and put this nightmare behind them.

But minutes went by. And more minutes. And more. Finally Mary untied the hammock ropes and sat up. The front of the *tienda* was stacked with the bright woven tapestries Stefani had been looking for all week. She's shopping! Mary thought. Damn her, she's shopping, and Seth is haggling, and they'll be in there for hours. She slipped down the side of the car, into the driver's seat, pulled the extra set of keys from the glove compartment, started the engine and drove off. She did not permit herself to laugh for miles, but once she started, she could not stop. She could picture the kids when they came out and found the car gone. They'd think "some Mexican" had stolen it with her dead body on top. They would start to argue about whose fault it was.

Mine! Mary thought exultant. Mine, all mine!

She'd give anything to see their faces. But that was the trouble with being dead: You couldn't hang around and enjoy things. She'd just have to head back to the resort with the lily lake, clean herself up, buy some pretty clothes, and find that good looking boatman. Then she'd call her lawyer back in the States, get her will changed, buy a house up here in the mountains and settle down, at last, to the life she had always meant to live.

Dumped: Seven Cautionary Tales

Bob and Betty

It was a good divorce. They each took one of the cars and one of the labradoodles; they divided the silver, antiques, and paintings, put the house up for sale, agreed to split the proceeds, and were shaking hands goodbye when they heard a musical tinkle from the garden. "Oh-oh," she remembered, "my wind chimes." "My wind chimes," he corrected. They hurried across the lawn and reached for the chimes at the exact same moment; when she tripped him, he slugged her, when he slugged her, she bit him. The realtor found their bodies later, chimes twined around their throats.

Gina and George

They fell in love the minute they met. He divorced his wife and she divorced her husband and they ran off to Paris together. For three weeks they left their hotel room only to eat in elegant restaurants, drink champagne, and take long walks in the soft spring rain. Nestled in his arms, she said, "I have never been so happy." He didn't answer. She kissed his eyelids, ran her finger along the deep crease in his forehead. "What's the matter?" she teased. "Aren't you happy too?"

"I would be," he said, "if I just had someone to talk to."

Dana and David

They lived on the same street, which was ideal, because they were both in their forties and they could see each other when they wanted and have their privacy when they wanted and anyway they were both so busy with their jobs and their friends and their children that it was good they didn't smother each other, and this went on until the afternoon her gas line exploded and he phoned to say he'd noticed the ambulance outside her house as he drove past and would have stopped but he'd had a conference call to make and was she okay?

Viv and Vince

They were in her favorite restaurant discussing the plans for their wedding. The food was hot, the wine was cold, but the service was slow. He joked about it; she did not. They had plenty of time, he said, their whole lives were before them, so what did it matter if the check was late? He watched her twist her engagement ring. Don't do it, he thought—but she did— she raised her arm, snapped her fingers, and whistled for the waitress. He had no choice. He rose, kissed her goodbye, and walked out.

Dumped: Seven Cautionary Tales

Kim and Krishna

She went trekking in Nepal and became infatuated with her Sherpa—a bright and eager young man who spoke perfect English. He was so curious about America that she invited him to come live with her in Berkeley. She would educate him, she said, she would put him through the university and see that he had a successful career. She sent him some money for new clothes and a ticket but when she saw him step off the plane in ostrich skin boots, a cowboy hat, and a white leather suit she slipped through the crowd and drove home alone.

Tom and Tilde

He had married the old woman for her money, so perhaps it served him right that for the next twenty years he had to wait on her hand and foot. When she finally died, her will stipulated that he would not get a single cent until he returned her ashes to Munich, the place of her birth. Learning it was illegal to bring human ashes into Germany, he carefully baked them into a loaf of black bread, wrapped it, packed it, and when the plane landed he took a taxi to the riverbank and fed her to the ducks.

Sean and Susan

She said the new baby might not be his. He backed the car over her cat. She gained sixty pounds. He cried out his ex-wife's name when he came. She sold his Ted Williams baseball bat for five dollars at a garage sale. He went to Bangkok for two weeks without her. She corrected his boss's grammar at a company dinner. He kissed her sister on the lips. She kissed his father on the lips. He drove off and left her at a truck stop. She found some pot in his sock drawer and threw it out. They're still together.

Life Cycle of a Tick

She stood at the window of the small airport and watched him cross the tarmac. He was the last one off. He had dyed his hair for this visit but he was wearing the same faded jeans and brown windbreaker he wore to work. She tapped the glass and waved but he kept his head down. She knew his bunion ached, his shoulder hurt, his hip pinched, and he was probably fibrillating after the cross-country flight. But still. He could look happier. It had been six weeks since they'd been together. She'd flown back to see him in San Francisco three times already. This was the first time he'd come to Arkansas to see her.

She joined the others waiting in the baggage area. Two Chinese pianists, brothers, were greeted by a claque of excited women from the town arts council. A young girl with a jagged haircut and a silver ball in her lower lip hopped up and down like a child as a soldier in uniform stepped forward to hug her. Local people with soft southern voices embraced, helped each other with baggage, exchanged news of family and friends, laughed. He alone—her long-term, long-distance lover—lagged. Had he decided to stay on the tarmac? He did not emerge until the room was almost empty. Then, with his duffel bag slung over his shoulders, he slouched through the doorway. He might be an old foot soldier returning from some foreign war. Or heading toward one. She opened her arms.

His hug was preemptory, his kiss on her forehead brusque, and the first thing he said was, "Boy, those are little planes. I wonder how often they go down."

"Every day. Yours is the first plane to get here in one piece in a year."

"You joke but you should hear the engines on those things. Kaputputput."

"Hi darling. Say hi darling."

He kissed her again, again on the forehead. "Don't want to give you my cold." He blew his nose on a napkin with an airplane logo on it and tucked it back in his pocket. "Although it may not be a cold," he mused as they stepped out into the bright afternoon. "They say this is the allergy capital of North America."

"Don't tell the natives that. They think it's the allergy capital of the world."

She opened the trunk of her car for his bag, helped him push the passenger seat back so he could stretch his legs, and pulled out of the parking lot. "Getting used to the humidity, aren't you," he said, as he fiddled with the air conditioner. "You've been here long enough."

She heard the hurt in his voice and didn't answer. She knew he was angry at her for renewing her contract with the arts museum. She should have talked to him about it before she agreed, but she was in the middle of a huge project and had said yes right away. He should understand. He knew how important it was to have work you enjoyed. He'd been unhappy with his construction firm for as long as she'd known him. She watched as he popped open the glove compartment and peered inside.

"My gun's behind the Bible in back," she explained.

He looked at her, startled, then reached over and started to massage her shoulder with such authority she almost veered off the road. He gave the world's best shoulder rubs. She had just begun to relax into his familiar touch when, ignoring the meadows, forests, and farmhouses outside his window he paused to put his ear to the dashboard. "Oh-oh," he said. "Your alternator. Can you hear it?"

"That's just the sound the engine makes."

"You ought to take it in and get it checked.'

"I did. It's fine."

"Who'd you take it to? Some big ole boy or a real mechanic?"

"Please? Give it a rest."

He didn't care for her new car but at least he liked her new apartment. He walked around inspecting it and when she asked, he agreed that the southwest view from the picture windows offered a nice slice of sunset. He was glad she had been able to manage the move from the other, smaller apartment in town on her own and he was sorry that he had been too busy to fly back and help with the packing. He tinkered with her dishwasher for ten minutes and fixed it; he helped her hang a heavy antique mirror she'd been unable to lift, and he adjusted the lock on her front door. He ate the cheese grits, okra and barbecued ribs she'd cooked half as a joke and half because she was beginning to love southern food, and he did not complain. He talked about his health, mentioned mutual friends, reminisced about a backpacking trip she and he had once taken through Mexico. He did not ask about her recent promotion, her projects, or her colleagues at the museum. He slept beside her in her bed, but he did not touch her.

Over breakfast the next morning he marveled about all the fat people he'd seen on the plane and asked, as he asked every time he saw her, if she'd bought a Confederate flag yet. He'd be happy to hoist it for her. It would look mighty good on that hanging tree down by the holler, yee haw.

"Are you done?" she asked. "Can you stop now?"

But he couldn't. She took him to the farmers market on the square and as they walked through the stalls of daffodils and spring onions he wondered how much of this was a front for the real commerce of marijuana farms and meth houses and he asked in a loud voice if she understood that eight out of ten people in this state were armed. She introduced him to her assistant and listened as he explained he could not shake hands because of his cold. "It must be lonely for him here," he murmured, after Peter left. Meeting her puzzled gaze, he added, "Being gay." She laughed. "Peter's not..." she began but he shushed her with a raise of his eyebrows. "Just because someone has good manners?" she pursued. He didn't answer. He noted there were no Blacks and few Asians in the market and he wanted to know where the Ku Klux Klan had their headquarters. Wasn't it nearby? Wasn't a town near here almost wiped out last winter from flashfloods? Snakes swim. Did she know that? Snakes survived floods by looping themselves over tree limbs. She should be very careful going anywhere near the river after a flood; she should always check the tree limbs.

"We're going to the river this afternoon," she reminded him.

"That's different," he said. "I'll be with you."

On the drive to the river he talked about microbes capable of killing the entire human population. He talked about the depletion of natural resources, the hole in the ozone, polar melt, acid rain, school shootings, terrorist attacks, toxins in meat and insect-borne diseases. He asked if she owned a tick extractor and when she said she did not he went into a convenience store to buy her one and picked one up for himself as well. He read every word from an insert in the box called The Life Cycle of a Tick as she drove. Nothing kills them, he announced. They swim even faster than snakes. They can survive freezing temperatures and scalding water, they live through entire washing machine cycles, they crawl out of fireplaces, nest in frozen pipes. They cause Anaplasmosis, Babesiosis, and Ehrlichiosis as well as Lyme. He closed his eyes with a deep sigh and when she looked over she saw he had fallen asleep. She thought of her desk at the museum, overflowing with work she longed to get back to, and wondered why she'd ever thought he'd like it here.

It was a long drive to the river town. The canoe they rented for their float sprang a leak almost at once and he banged his knuckles on a submerged rock as he helped her bail. "Sure can hurt yourself having a good time," he said as they rowed back to the take-out. The guide at the rental place gave them a map of hiking trails nearby and showed them where to find Indian caves and the meadow where elk grazed. "I hear elk can get pretty mean," her lover offered, and the guide obliged by saying, "Yeah, but what you really got to watch out for are the mountain lions."

"And the poison ivy," she added as they set out on the widest trail. "And slipping off a sheer limestone bluff into a rattlesnake cave filled with nettles only to be attacked by fire ants and eaten alive by a bear that you manage to beat off with an armadillo which ends up giving you leprosy."

"Funny," he said, when she finished.

Their motel room reeked of bug spray and the fan ran noisily all night. Once again, citing his cold, he lay beside her like a brother, without touching. But in the morning, over chicken and waffles in a sunny cafe, he agreed she had brought him to a sweet place and though he knew the surrounding hills harbored nothing but killer dog packs, crazed Christian cults, and armed drug lords he was willing to walk around the town and admire the stone post office and hand-built houses. He paused before the courtyard of an old hotel. "There's your bear," he said. She laughed, but looked where he pointed. At first she saw nothing but a tire swinging back and forth. But then she saw the enormous bear squatting in its cage. "Third generation in captivity," she read out loud. "Kisses children. Plays the guitar."

"Rips your head off," he added.

She stared at the bear. Melon colored nose, dark reddish fur, satisfied bright eyes that did not meet hers. Despite herself, she shivered.

It was too cold to try the river again so they drove up the mountain instead and stopped at a viewpoint. A telescope was planted near the cliff edge but it was surrounded by thigh-high grasses that looked, he said, "seriously dangerous." Copperheads, he elaborated. Brown recluses. Ticks, of course, everywhere. And chiggers. She was tired and didn't protest. They unrolled their windows, breathed in the fresh air, looked out at the mauve hills and masses of trees leafing out below, and listened to the birds. She had been taking long solitary walks on the weekends, she told him, trying to identify native birds by their songs. The red cardinals had a commanding whistle and the cedar waxwings had a lispy trill but, "Look!" she cried. "An eagle!" She pointed to the swift shadow passing over the valley below and threw open her door to stand outside and get a better look. "We have bald eagles here!" she exulted, turning to see her lover, arms crossed, still sitting inside the car.

"We?" he repeated.

She stared. "What is the matter with you?"

"Just didn't reckon you'd go native so fast."

"I haven't gone na..."

"Sure coulda fooled me."

"Coulda? Look if you didn't want me to move here you could have said so."

"And you would have listened?"

"You could have asked me to stay. You never once asked me to stay."

"Why? You were only going to 'try' this job. Remember? Try it for a while and then come back. You can't be happy here."

"Why not?" she snapped. "It's a great job and it's better than..." she stopped, took a deep breath. "You were going to 'try' to retire and join me here, remember?"

"Looks like we both need to try a little harder."

We? she thought, but did not say.

They drove farther up the twisting road and stopped to look at willow baskets and corncob pipes in a souvenir shop. The owner wanted to tell them about the winter before. It had been so icy cows slipped and fell and the ice was so hard the cows' bones pierced right through them and they died by the dozen. Her lover turned to her. "Did you hear that?" Worst December ever, the owner nodded. Doing his genealogy, the owner continued, he'd recently learned his wife was related to a Davis and he checked and sure enough it was Jefferson. "Did you hear that?" her lover asked, his voice dark and sly. She shrugged, bought pralines made by the man's wife: Brown sugar, pecans, butter—no preservatives, no chemicals—and ate half a pound by herself in the car, while her lover took photos of the owner and his three-legged hound dog to show, he said, his friends back home.

She had made a reservation at a touristy lakeside lodge for them that night but she had neglected to make a reservation for dinner and when they arrived that afternoon they were told they would have to eat elsewhere. They unpacked in their cottage under the redbuds and then set out again. "Lookit all dem churches," he marveled. "Guess y'all need 'em here with all yer shotgun weddins and family feud funerals 'n all." He leaned out the window and started to hack.

"Don't spit," she warned, her voice sharp enough to surprise them both. He pulled the airplane napkin out of his shirt pocket and coughed into it showily for the rest of the drive. At the diner he mocked the menu, reading the items out loud in a redneck sing-song, but then ordered deep-fried catfish, hush puppies, biscuits with gravy, and blackberry cobbler with cinnamon ice cream. He ate every bite and winked at her as he finished, lips slicked with grease. "Purty good eatin'," he said as he rose to find a "two-holer" in back.

Had he always been so awful? She watched him walk away, a tall man, getting old but still good looking, with the wary grace that had always thrilled her. She had met him at an outdoor concert thirteen years ago. He had been raising three teenage boys at the time and she had been caring for her elderly mother, but the idea of living together someday had always been there. If he loved her—did he love her?—he'd be living with her now. Why wasn't he? He'd do well here. He could follow his old dream of just doing woodwork. Coward, she thought, and then, No, it's me. I'm the coward. I'm the one who ran away. She flicked her glass of iced tea with her finger, remembering the night after work when Peter and Peter's wife had come to christen her new apartment with a jar of moonshine. When Peter's wife, a little tipsy, had asked why she'd left California she'd lied, babbled on about the career opportunities at the new museum, the pay raise, the low cost of living, never once admitting how badly she had wanted a change, any change, how frightened she'd been of staying stuck in the same place in her old life forever.

"How's your cold?" she asked, forcing a smile when he returned.

"Better." He smiled back at her for the first time.

That night they made love and although her lover didn't come, he was tender. She nuzzled into his chest as she always had, and when she asked he said yes he had missed her and yes he was glad to be here; he just wished she'd come back to the

West Coast, where she belonged. They fell asleep entwined in each other's arms and woke hours later to a huge bang of thunder. Lightning flared, followed by rain in swift hard sweeps, then hail. "Tornado," he decided, excited. He got up to see if they could both fit in the bathtub, if it came to that, because bathtubs were the safest place to be in tornadoes, and then he stood by the window, his silhouette like a petrograph of a caveman, round head on a triangle back, stick arms lifted. When the storm stilled, he pulled on his clothes and stepped outside, where he was joined by other men, from other cottages, all talking in the same excited voices. A tree had fallen, she heard, right through the roof of the lodge's restaurant, the place where they had been lucky enough not to eat last night. Some cars had been damaged by blowing debris. A pet dog had run off but a ranger had found it and brought it back.

She reached for the pillow that smelled of him, of musk and cough drops, and hugged it close, wishing it could make her feel whole; she had not felt whole in a long time. She must have fallen asleep again for in her dream she was alone in a stalled plane and the word on her lips when she awoke was the word he'd said when he'd first arrived: kaput.

She shook her head to clear it, took a shower and was dressed by the time her lover came back in, rosy, full of news about the storm and about the men he had met down at the emergency café set up by the lodge. She smiled to see him—that handsome face she had missed so much—but her smile faded when she saw he was holding a single cardboard cup of coffee. He had not brought anything for her? "All you think about is yourself," she said calmly. "You never think about us, as a couple. I would never buy a coffee without buying you one too."

"We can share."

"How? I take my coffee black, remember."

"I didn't come all this way to fight with you."

"What did you 'come all this way' for?"

"Right." He reached for his duffle bag and yelped as a large striped scorpion dropped out, scurried across the floor, skipped beneath his boot heel and disappeared under the bed. He turned, his face dark with triumph. "See?" he crowed, and for a second she hated him. If only she could keep on hating him. If only things were that easy. She bent, pushed the flimsy bed aside with both hands and stomped on the scorpion twice with her sandal.

"C'mon," she said, furious, slinging her own bag over her shoulder. "We're going to be late."

"Late for what?"

"Didn't the boys down at the lodge tell you? There's going to be a lynching at noon. Tickets only, but I got us front seats."

"Ha ha," he said, weary. But he followed her out to the car and they drove in silence for twenty minutes before she pulled off to the side of the road by a strip mall and crept into his lap and sobbed while he rocked her back and forth in his strong, impatient arms.

Ram and Dam

Summers, now that the kids are gone, Glen and I take the dog and drive out to the cabin on the lake. We stay all weekend. Glen has carpentry projects and the boat to keep him busy, but I don't have that much to do. The cabin doesn't have running water and we still use the outhouse—you can get used to anything, I guess—so a lot of my time is taken up with basic maintenance. I knock the cobwebs down from the rafters and wash the windows and rake the path through the oak trees and sweep up around the wood stove and do the dishes; to scour the cast iron skillet in lake water I have to squat on the limestone shelf, a chore that always makes me feel like an Osage squaw. Kidnapped! Sold to an old white man! Soon, Glen says, we'll have running water but Glen's been saying "soon" for the last twenty years and the word has lost its meaning.

I always bring work from the office and lots of library books but I rarely touch them. I swim; I take photos of the eagles; I groom the dog for ticks; I keep an eye out for copperheads; I knit. Mostly I lie out on the boat dock and watch the water. The light on the lake is ever-changing—a silky pink at dawn, a tawny tea at mid-morning (so clear you can see the gold eyes of the sunfish swirling under the pier posts), chopped liver at noon when the power boats whiz by, hammered pewter at two, tropical blue at four, a bowl of bronze as the sun sets.

Friends drop by from time to time, not as many as used to; the lake has changed, more young people now. Patti and Dodge pull their boat up to the dock to visit but Dodge can be drunk by noon and Patti has had a stroke, which makes it hard for her to talk, though she does like to sit and have her hand held. The crazy millionaire who bought up most of the south shore blows his bugle as he passes and the two gay college professors bring their guitars over to drink beer and jam with Glen on his fiddle.

In the late afternoon after everyone's left I might take a walk—the dog loves that and darts ahead of me—and we go up through the woods to the limestone bluffs to see the east side of the lake shining bright through the cedars. I always go to the very edge of the cliff and crouch to peer over to the limestone ledge beneath. The dog won't follow me there but I need to see how my wild goats are doing. There are two of them—the old ram, dead since December, but regal as a pharaoh, kneels on the ledge facing the lake, nothing left of him now but bone and horns and hanks of black and silver hair, no smell even, and his young dam stands guard beside him, sometimes turning her head to look at me with alien yellow eyes. I admire her for her loyalty and fear for her loneliness and I always say, "Stay safe" before I back away and leave.

Glen and I usually watch the sunset from the boat, motor turned off, drifting in the middle of the lake. Swallows dart and swoop around us; small mouth bass jump just out of casting reach; geese bray from the other shore. We take the iPad, so we can hear our favorite bluegrass show. Glenn sips Jack Daniels from his coffee cup, I sip red wine from a thermos. We watch the sky cook—it goes from pale scrambled yolks to hot burnt apricot jam to stovetop black when the stars come out. Wild honeysuckle wafts from the shore and the lake waters offer up their good stinks of gasoline and fish. When "The Pickin' Post" is over we dock the boat and walk back up through the woods to the cabin. I cook our dinners on the camp stove—nothing fancy, just our usual standbys, spaghetti, venison chili, sometimes catfish or crappie, if Glenn's caught any, and we eat on the porch by the light from the Coleman lantern. We talk—not much—I know he's worried about his prostate, though the tests show his cancer's in remission, and he knows I'm worried about our oldest, who has moved to Kansas City with yet another loser—but we spare each other our re-runs and stay still. Sometimes we share a joint. Glen plays his fiddle in the dark—"The Ashokan Farewell," my favorite, it always breaks my heart even though he flubs the same chords every time—and "The Gardenia Waltz," which, if I'm high enough, I'll dance to. Then we push the dog down to the end of the futon, check the flannel sheets for brown recluses, make love if we're lucky and fall asleep.

I do not want to dream about the wild goats but sometimes I do anyway and when I open my eyes to the night and hear the soft sounds of the woods and the lake and the owls and the hunting foxes spilling secretly, beautifully, all around us, I have to hold my breath to bite back the terror. Nothing lasts, I know that. I turn to Glen and put my arm around his shoulder, gently, so as not to wake him but once his apnea sets in I don't bother being gentle and give his back such a good smack he sits up and smacks me right back and then we both lie there and laugh until we can't laugh anymore and it's time to get up, light the camp stove for coffee, and start a new day.

Harm Done

The couple upstairs screamed at each other all night and the couple downstairs wept. I was fascinated by their troubles and often crouched in my nightgown by the heater vent that ran through the center of our triplex, listening. The problems upstairs had to do with drinking, I discovered; the problems downstairs had to do with cheating. My young husband and I were the only happy couple in the building. I smiled as I came back one night, slipped into our bed, and cuddled close. I had scarcely closed my eyes before I heard the words: *Kill him.*

I sat up. The words had not come from above or below. The words were my own and the man I was speaking to stood in the bedroom doorway. He was a stranger to me, tall and stoop-shouldered. It was too dark to see his face. But I could see he held a gun.

Kill him, I repeated. I pointed to the pillow where my husband lay with one bare arm flung over his head and his smooth throat exposed. The stranger approached, leaned over, pressed the gun against my husband's heart and fired. There was no sound but my husband's chest opened like a flower. His eyes

96

opened too. He turned to me. "Honey?" he asked. Blood pooled from his parted lips.

I leapt out of bed. There had been a mistake. "We have to get him to a hospital," I chattered. "Hurry! We have to get him to the hospital at once."

The stranger nodded, propped my husband up, and led him out the hall and down the front stairs to a car parked on the street below. Just before they drove away my husband turned to look up at me through the car window. His expression was serene and sweetly loving. There was no blame in it.

I collapsed to my knees in gratitude. My husband would live. The doctors would save him. No harm had been done. And then I saw that the car was not going to the hospital. It was going the other way, out to the country. This stranger was not going to save my husband. He was going to do what I'd asked him to do. He was going to kill him.

I woke up in terror. It was dawn; the house was silent; my husband slept beside me. I touched his chest. It was warm and firm and intact. His heart beat innocently beneath my hand. He stirred and turned and reached for me. I settled back down beside him but I kept my eyes open and as soon as it was light I slipped out of bed and went into the kitchen and cooked his favorite breakfast and brought it back to him on a tray.

Six months later a tall stooped stranger said my name at a neighborhood party. He stood in a doorway with the light behind him and when I turned he kissed me. We became lovers and after a year of terrible lies I divorced my husband, who was angry at first, but not that hurt; he soon bought a sports car, began dating twenty-year-olds and took a better job in a more glamorous city. I was less fortunate. My affair with the stranger didn't last. There was always something wrong between us. Something he knew nothing about. Something I could never forgive.

Violations

At night Anna can see into the apartment directly across the
street. The young woman who lives there is in trouble and
Anna is concerned. When the girl weeps at the window, Anna
wants to stretch her hand out her own window and console
her, but Anna is confined to her bed on the sixth floor of The
Haven, strapped upright to her mattress. Not all the attendants
speak English and those who do don't believe her when she ex-
plains that a girl is being brutally raped night after night in the
building right across from them. The night nurse, the one from
Jamaica, politely leans forward to listen, his breath sweet with
spiced rum, but then, less politely, he laughs. His lips move.
"How can you see across the street?" she imagines him teasing.
"You are ninety-six years old. Your eyes are that good?"

Yes. Anna's vision is perfect. Her hearing went years ago but
she can still see; she can still read, not like she used to, none of
the Russians or her beloved Shakespeare; these days she reads
only the paperbacks that the orderlies leave behind. The stories
are junk but they give Anna something to think about during
the short days and interminable nights. "We need to help that
girl," she urges the nurse.

Violations

The nurse sways gracefully to the window and peers through the bars. He turns with a shrug and a smile and draws two lines in the air. Anna understands. The curtain on the girl's apartment is closed. Of course. It's early. "The red-haired man doesn't come until midnight," she remembers. The nurse nods, pries Anna's mouth open with a firm finger, places the pills on her tongue and holds the water cup gently, allowing her to sip. Some of the other attendants force the pills down her throat, not caring if she chokes. The red-haired man sometimes chokes the girl, comes up behind her and grips her neck, lifts her until her little feet dangle and then he pulls the front of her dress down so her boobies pop out and plunges himself inside her while she fights for breath. Sometimes he handcuffs and gags her, sometimes he throws her over the couch or face-down to the floor. It is a terrible thing to watch. Terrible. And yet, when he comes in the door the girl smiles and when he leaves she begs him to stay.

"Can you explain that?" Anna asks the priest. The priest is coal black, from Africa, and he doesn't even try to answer, which is a relief, because the two priests before him thought there were answers to everything. This one simply smiles, passes a hand over her face and moves down the ward. "Why would anyone..." she stops, for the foot of her bed is being shaken by a wild-haired man in a housedress who is glaring at her, tongue stuck out, "choose to be violated?"

The old man spits at her.

"Nurse!" Anna watches the man through narrowed eyes and clutches her doll until the wretch wanders off. The worst thing about being old, she knows, is being around other old people. Everyone on her ward is insane. The doll, no more than a few twists Anna has made in a white cotton handkerchief, bows in agreement, and Anna tucks her back in the folds of the blanket where she will be safe. She does not know how long she has had this particular doll or when it will be discovered and thrown into the laundry like the rest. She is determined not to mourn.

What she cannot determine to do is not worry. When did simple lovemaking get so savage? Anna's three husbands had been gentle men. Too gentle? Had she wanted to be kicked and beaten, to have her bottom slapped, her nipples pinched, to have her hair pulled and her clothes torn off? Well, she thinks, with a short harsh laugh, I should have come to The Haven earlier then. I should have demanded enemas and syringes when I was sexy enough to enjoy them. She touches the long soft flap of her breast under the flowered yellow nightgown the night nurse is putting her in. She tries to tell him it is not her nightgown, that it belongs to some other old lady, but pulling her arms through one by one he only shrugs as if to say, "It's yours now," so whoever it once belonged to must have died. Lucky. She lets herself be tied down for the night, feels the nurse's cool touch brush something wet off her cheek. Tears? Irritated that she cannot use her own hands, she twists her face on the pillow, and waits.

The curtain opens at twelve o'clock and the lights go on as usual, turning the room into a lit stage, but the girl, for once, is alone. She has a pale childlike body that is totally hairless—a fact that has amazed Anna although she vaguely remembers reading about a waxy cleft like the girl's in one of her paperbacks; her long dark hair is parted down the middle, her face is round and plain. The bites on her neck are still visible and the cut under her eye still bleeds. Anna waits for the girl to do something, to open the wine, plump up the pillows. But the girl stands in the center of the room, as still as a shop mannequin, and Anna sees for the first time that the door behind her has been bolted and locked. The knob rattles wickedly back and forth. The red-haired man must be out in the hallway, roaring to come in. Anna strains against her bed straps. Good for you!

Violations

Anna cries to the girl. Keep him out! The girl pivots to stare straight at Anna across the dark divide of the street. She points a tattooed finger. Dirty old cunt, she says. You keep him out.

Shocked, Anna closes her eyes. When she awakes the apartment across the street is curtained again. Maybe it always was. Anna neither knows nor cares. Morning sunlight pours through the window bars onto her bedtable with its faded photos and artificial geraniums. "God has forgotten me," Anna says to the Filipina who replaces the Jamaican at dawn. The Filipina has heard this before. She pulls the bedpan out and Anna lets herself be roughly lifted and dropped back upon the unclean sheets. Tonight, Anna realizes, no brute drama will play out across the street. There will be nothing to move her to revulsion, arousal, or pity. There will be no one to worry about, no one to hate, no one to care for. She sighs and reaches for her doll. Tonight, she realizes, might be the longest night of her life.

Not a Cupid

I bought him from a woman in Juarez who said she was his aunt. She said his name was Beto; she said he was twelve. He didn't look twelve; he looked ten, a black-eyed brat with curly hair and scabby knees. His smile was sweeter than the others I'd bought and I was surprised when he took my hand. He did not look back at the woman when we left, though I turned and for a long time her image stayed in my mind. She was leaning against the bus station wall with my money shoved in her jeans pocket crying *Gracias* to the clouds in an exhausted voice.

Juarez is a dangerous town but I had my knife and Beto and I walked safely through the crowded streets to my hotel. Are you hungry? I asked in my bad Spanish. Do you want to stop and eat? Shall I buy you new clothes? Shall we go to the amusement park? Would you like an ice cream? He smiled, that sweet smile, but said nothing. His hand in mine was small and hot and firm.

The minute we entered my room, Beto pulled his tee shirt off and stepped out of his shorts. Surprised, I took in his narrow chest and the thin wings of his shoulders. He tugged my hand as if to lead me toward the bed but I knelt and explained there had been a mistake. I had asked for a child, not a cupid. Had the aunt misunderstood? Beto, still smiling, cupped my chin and kissed me, mouth open, slack, damp, his small bundle of manhood innocently a-droop. When I cried No and pushed back, he disappeared into the kitchen, returning with a glass of fresh milk. He sat at my feet as I thought what to do. The milk was cold and sweet and soothing. Too soothing. Drugged, I slumped onto the floor.

When I came to, I was gagged and bound and Beto was at my breasts, sucking like a little monkey. He could not be disengaged and despite myself I gurgled in horrified satisfaction. His thin fingers were everywhere, in my ears, my nostrils, my mouth, my cunt, my anus, strong and nimble and quick and unpleasant. He seemed to have no sense of what was erotic and what was not and I was by turns aroused, irritated, bored, and brought into unwelcome explosions of pleasure. He licked my armpits, scratched my neck, nibbled my knees, peeled strips off my sunburned shoulders, made my navel a cup for his warm spit. He was, during all this time, limp. And why not? He was a child! What was my woman's body to him? A soccer field, a swimming pool, a tree to climb, an alley to run through, a drum to beat, a guitar to strum and pluck—a playground. I too went limp. And that is when the tickling started. The terrible tickling! How Beto laughed when I writhed on the floor and helplessly farted! How he crowed with delight when my bladder succumbed.

This went on for hours. He was not unkind. He dressed and undressed me, draped me in jewelry, fed me candy and soda pop. He drew rockets and robots on my skin with red lipstick, he braided my hair, painted my toenails, he pinched and poked and covered my face with his damp sucky kisses until he too at last tired.

Not a Cupid

Only then, as I lay in a puddle of my own urine did he nestle close, his little head on my breast, his hand curled between my legs. I had not been this close to another human being in a long time, I realized; I had traveled alone for years and only now knew how I had missed having someone to hold and be held by. Beto shivered in his sleep, and I rested my chin against the top of his head, breathing in his unwashed salty young boy stench, and sang what I could remember of an old lullaby. I will not use my knife on this one I thought. This one I will save. This one I will keep. It will take some time, but this one I will teach.

Celtic Studies

Whether from bad timing, bad luck, or bad judgment, Meg McCarty woke up the morning of her forty-sixth birthday convinced that the one thing she wanted was a husband. Her friends tried to talk her out of it. A group of handsome, hard-working, independent women, most were divorced or content being single. Not Meg. Her elderly parents had just died and left her some money. She did not want a cat. She did not want a gay friend. She did not want a sports car. She wanted a permanent man in her life.

"You'll never find one in San Francisco," her friends warned.

Meg suspected this was correct. She began to look at other cities, other states, other countries. One day at work, fooling around on her office computer, she opened a blog on Ireland. It claimed that Irish men liked women. That was unusual enough to make Meg read on. It seemed that Irish men were devoted to their mothers, loyal to their sisters, proud of their daughters, and faithful to their wives. Rape statistics were low; spousal battery statistics were low. A shiver ran through her. She researched further. The men her age in Dublin were mostly married businessmen, the men her age in Cork were mostly married shop owners, but the men in Galway were mostly un-married and many—Galway was a university town on the west coast—were scholars, poets, and artists.

"Romantics," Meg mused. She wrote the university and en-rolled in a summer course. She took a leave from the ad agency, sublet her apartment, and said goodbye to her skeptical friends, most of whom, with straight faces, asked to be invited to the wedding. With such an absence of irony that they feared for her, Meg said, "You will be," and took off on Aer Lingus.

She had packed flimsy new underwear and sturdy new walk-ing shoes but she did not remember she'd forgotten her um-brella until the plane landed in rain at Shannon Airport. That was all right; she would simply ask some unattached male to share an umbrella with her. She had always been shy but the time for shyness was past.

The first Irishman she met was the customs official. He had merry eyes, a tuft of sparse beard, and ringless fingers. "McCa-rty," he mused, examining her passport. "Now tell me, love, how Irish are ye?"

"Both sides," Meg lied. She had dyed her hair red for this trip and bought green contact lenses which made her eyes wa-ter in a way she hoped was appealing. She brushed a tear aside and bit down so hard on her single dimple it hurt.

"And how many generations would that be?"

"How many generations what?"

"Since ye emigrated."

"Two?"

Wrong answer. The customs man tugged his tuft and waved her on. Dismissed, Meg dropped her passport back into her purse. On the way out she saw the little boy she'd held on her lap during most of the flight. He waved, shy and joyful. He had stayed awake all night with her, looking at the moon shining over the Atlantic.

"We're here," he whispered, as if sharing a secret. "In Ireland!"

"Yes!" She bent to give him the last roll of lifesavers in her coat pocket. "Ireland!"

As she straightened, she wondered what "Ireland" meant to him, a six-year-old kid traveling alone—a plate of cookies waiting on his grandparents' kitchen table? A fishing trip to Galway Bay? She scanned the crowd. He might have an interesting uncle—Ireland was full of bachelor uncles—but the boy was picked up, hugged, and carried off by two teenaged girls. Turning, she saw one of the flight attendants pass by, pulling his suitcase. He had a model's uninteresting beauty—even features, mild tan, white teeth—and he nodded to her with a regal dip of his sleek head. She remembered how useless he'd been on the plane, spilling hot coffee on her as he chatted with another attendant, and how, twice, he'd forgotten to bring the boy's milk. She did not nod back.

Instead, she hefted her own suitcase with its brave festoon of green ribbon off the baggage carousel and reset her watch. The quiet throb in her left ovary made itself felt again, a small pain that had been sounding its warning the last few months. She waited for it to pass, then ran lip gloss over her dry lips, rearranged her cleavage, and approached three men one at a time to ask directions for the Galway bus stop. The three could have been cousins. Neither handsome nor plain, they were uniformly pale, with a moist sheen to their beardless faces. They had light eyes, light hair. Their beauty lay in their voices, sweet and lilting, as each in turn pointed in a different direction and said, "You can't miss it."

Meg got the correct directions from a girl at the Information Desk and headed outside.

The bald man waiting in the rain at the shelter was not exactly hostile when she asked (again) if this was the right stop for Galway; simply jabbing at the schedule right in front of her could be seen as helpful. She smiled once or twice to get his attention but he stared into the distance, smoking, and so she resorted to silence herself, which could be seen as mysterious.

Rain flattened her hair and ran down the inside of her collar. The man preceded her onto the bus (the driver was a woman) and turned toward the window; she was about to sit next to him but that seat was claimed by an old lady who pulled out a rosary and began to kiss it with a furtive aggression that was too private to watch. Meg settled farther back, beside a freckled schoolgirl who held her cell phone as if it too were a holy object, looking down at it with lips moving in her own silent prayer, one Meg knew well, *Please let him call me Please let him call me.*

Meg turned her attention to the window. Green fields, brown cows, white daisies, low stone walls. Would her intended live on a farm? He'd be good with horses and give thrilling massages. Or maybe He'd live in a small town like the one the bus was passing through now, in one of those cottages with a yellow door and a yard overgrown with poppies. Or perhaps He was a wealthy physician, summering in that stone house, half hidden in woods. "How do you know 'He' even exists?" her friends had teased before she left and Meg had laughed because of course she didn't know. Ever since deciding to come, she'd been blessed with conviction and blinded to facts. All she knew was that she'd find Him here, somewhere, soon. She leaned back in the bus seat and woke up with a dry throat and drool on her chin when the bus stopped in Galway.

The cab driver, like the customs man, started off as flirtatious. "You're here for the university, are ye, love?" His voice was warm and tender, but he said nothing more after Meg volunteered that yes, she was taking a course in Celtic Studies. Was that the wrong thing to say? Was there a secret response she didn't know? These men! They threw the ball, she threw it back, they dropped it. The cab driver was good looking, about her age, pale, like all of them, and, like all of them, able to grant the first "love" and no other.

Of the town of Galway she saw little—a warren of gray streets around a torn-up main square. Her room was at the edge of the city, by the river, in a student housing complex with a Gaelic name she could not pronounce. She had agreed to share with three other Americans, all of whom, she suspected, would be years younger than she, but that was all right, she liked young people, and besides, she wouldn't be home much. She planned to spend her free time in the pubs, looking wistfully into an untouched Guinness until He approached and sat down beside her.

A few hours later, after a nap and a shower, that is exactly where she found herself, but the seat across from her was occupied by one of her housemates, Lydia, a nineteen-year-old from Tucson with cerebral palsy. "I can't carry my own books," Lydia was explaining. "I need help going up and down stairs and getting on and off buses. I have no peripheral vision." She stopped to give Meg the same gentle but commanding look Meg had received the last few years from her invalid parents. "Also, I can't really cook for myself."

"That's all right," Meg heard herself saying. "I'll cook for you."

Lydia gave a lopsided smile and stood up. She wore thick glasses but she had pure pink and white skin, like a girl dipped in rose milk, and a plump mouth sudsy with white teeth. She had large breasts and as she lurched away they plunged inside her tee shirt like fat puppies on leashes. She'll get laid before I do, Meg thought. "Don't worry," Lydia said, as if she were reading her mind. "This is the safest pub in Galway. In terms of men, I mean. They don't hit on you here."

And they didn't. Meg finished her drink, trying, by osmosis, to attract the two men beside her who were in deep discussion and even deeper agreement, nodding and encouraging each other, but what she heard ("There was a man hung himself in those woods back of Conneely's." "Why?" "Who knows! There was a tree!") had to have been a joke, and though she laughed appreciatively, neither man did.

Embarrassed to be caught eavesdropping, she slipped off her stool and walked outside. It was nine at night, but still light, so she left the town behind and walked down the river path. Lupine, wild roses, yellow iris and buttercups grew along the bank and the evening air smelled of sweet clover. Rounding a bend, she saw a ruined castle across the river, its stone turrets green with ivy, swallows darting through its open windows. Two actual swans swam by. The setting could not have been more perfect, and when she heard footsteps behind her she turned, prepared, only to waste her smile of welcome on a heavyset woman walking two brown and white spaniels. A neon green tennis ball bounced out of one of the dogs' mouths, and Meg, after a sullen moment, scooped it up and threw it back.

When Meg came back to the apartment, a bearded boy named Jeremy from Ohio, Lydia, and an excitable girl named Sheila were all watching television in the common room. They had found a Gaelic channel—an interview with a retired hurling champion, a man of sixty with thinning hair, a scar on his cheek and an expression of such quiet sorrow that Meg stood on after the others went out to the pubs again, fascinated. So this was a true Irish hero: the thin lips, clear eyes, grave voice saying, in the subtitles below, "The only thing I've ever loved in my whole life is this game."

Sad, Meg thought. She thought of all the things she'd loved, her parents, her friends, her books, photographs, music, even her job. The only love she'd never known was the constant love of one good man and that would come. She turned the TV off and went into her room, with its built-in desk and study lamp. She crawled into her narrow nun's cot, pressed a hand against her throbbing ovary, and slept for eleven hours, dreaming unhappily of the flight attendant.

Classes began the next day and Lydia led the way, lurching toward the university so recklessly that Meg had to rein her back from the traffic at every corner, while Jeremy in turn stopped traffic taking photographs to send home to his girlfriend, and Sheila, in a mini skirt, blew kisses to the furious drivers. Their professor met them at the door to their classroom and shook their hands as they entered. A few inches shorter than Meg, with a head of copper curls, a gold earring, and the broad chest of a weightlifter, Professor Riordan seemed unable to look anyone in the eye as he told them what books he'd "like" them to read, what lectures he "hoped" they'd attend, what outings he "prayed" they'd enjoy. He twisted his wedding ring as he spoke, worrying it back and forth. Perhaps, Meg thought, he was abashed by the presence of the three pretty blondes from San Diego in the center row, or by Lydia's tight tee shirt, or Sheila's bare knees, or maybe even by her, in her itchy Aran sweater and tam.

The afternoon session was taught by Dr. Shaughnessy, a thin man in a tweed suit who was supposed to talk about Irish history but instead spoke about the effects of fast food on the Irish diet and fast cars on the Irish roadways. For two hours he ranted against the speed economy that was killing language and literature, taking lives and ruining families. Meg liked his passion, and thanked him for the lecture after class, but with a sly look past her he gathered his papers and darted away, as long legged as a jack rabbit.

The next day's lecture was on literature: Professor Riordan, wringing his hands, quoted Yeats and Kavanagh. Wednesday's lecture, taught by a limp young man in sunglasses, was on the Celtic harp; Thursday's, taught by a married Chinese geologist, was on limestone, and Friday's, taught by a woman, was on film.

It was clear that any fantasies she might have entertained about dating an academic were doomed, but Meg thought about Dr. Shaughnessy's original lecture as she walked toward the center of town on Saturday morning. Hadn't she come to Ireland just for the reasons he insisted were obsolete? To meet a slow man at a slow pace, with time to ramble and ruminate? Her life in the States had been so crowded with work and the responsibility of nursing her two parents through their interminable cancers that she had not really had a chance to just... the word caught her up with pleasure... drift.

Drifting, she wove through the wet cobblestone streets fronted with sweater shops and craft shops and darkly recessed pubs, tipping the bad bagpipers and sloppy jugglers and quaking mimes, stepping aside for uniformed schoolgirls and tattooed teenagers and couples pushing prams. Outside the shops, volunteers stood in the rain collecting money for children in Africa and Iraq and Afghanistan and almost everyone stopped to give. Music poured from the pubs—American music mostly, songs Meg knew, "Cripple Creek" and "Proud Mary"—the smell of fish and chips spiked the air, and the river flowed fresh through banks lined with wildflowers.

She walked through light rain all day and at seven-thirty that evening found herself in front of the Town Hall Theater. She entered and bought a ticket for a play about a celibate farmer. It was a comedy and the audience laughed but Meg saw far too many parallels to her own situation. The poor farmer was loveless. He was balked and eventually defeated by the church, by the greed and guile of his friends, and by his own timidity. Though she clapped with the others, Meg left depressed, remembering how the actor playing the farmer wiped the sweat off his forehead as he exited and his lost look as he bowed. There had been something about that actor she liked—the same quiet male dignity she had liked in the hurling champion—and she scanned the program for his name. Tim McCarty. Imagine! Her last name! They might be related! Though probably not. Her father's family had intermarried with Germans, French, English, Scotch and Native American—anyone who would have them—and her mother's family had been Jewish.

The rain was falling hard when she came out of the theater and she hurried to catch the shuttle bus. There was one other passenger getting on, an old man who sat down behind the driver. "What a night!" she exclaimed as she climbed aboard.

"Desperate," the two men agreed. They were already deep into a joke of some sort and lowered their voices to shut her out; the old man's voice, however, had a dramatic timbre that carried and so Meg heard about the Irishman who had sex twice, twenty years apart, but not, thank God, with the same woman. What was so funny about that? She shrugged as the two men burst into laughter and the old man got off and loped away in his jeans and denim jacket.

The next morning Meg awoke to a strange and welcome silence: the absence of rain. She dressed and headed out to the river path, again besotted with the romance of the yellow furled iris, the reeds along the riverbank, the pink morning glory threading through the sunlit underbrush. Her foot accidentally brushed a stand of dandelions, and she stopped, arms lifted, as the pewter fluff floated around her like goblin soap bubbles. What a magical country. Smiling, she crouched under a willow shrub and looked into the shallows, where, for the first time, she noticed a generic eddy of garbage, beer bottles, cigarette butts and condoms; her smile left and she was stabbed with sadness. She had no business being here. Her quest was naïve. She was no longer young, she was orphaned, childless, and had had her heart broken too many times in too many places to even count. She pressed her hand to a throbbing ovary and walked back to cook breakfast for her housemates, who had already started to call her Mom.

She spent the following weeks being Mom, helping Lydia up the narrow stairs of Blarney Castle and holding her as she bent backwards to kiss the sleek green slab before lying down to kiss it herself. She extricated Sheila from a club where she was being fondled by an exultant drunk who cried, "And wouldn't you be a nice girl to keep in a back room!" She gave her phone card to Jeremy who needed to call his girlfriend in the States and she walked each of the three blondes home after they'd thrown up in pubs. She applied herself to her studies and gave up looking for Him. He, she thought, can look for me. She read, walked, explored, took a ferry to the Aran Islands and a bus to Kylemore Abbey, moving invisibly but not unhappily through the crowds of other tourists, couples, and students. She climbed the Cliffs of Moher and Yeats's tower, traveled to Dublin to admire the Book of Kells, and twice returned to the Town Theater to see Tim McCarty. If she could not find a man to love, at least she had found a country. Every evening she walked by the river in the late summer twilight, something Professor Riordan told her was called, beautifully, "the simmer dim." The sky was always alive with drama, clouds piling and parting, and the peace of the place, the kindness and courtesy of the people, comforted her.

On the last day of class she was in the supermarket buying groceries for her housemates' farewell dinner when she saw a familiar face. It was the white-haired old man she'd seen on the bus, only he wasn't that old and the white was a bleach job.

"Tim McCarty," she said. "I've been in love with you for weeks."

He turned to her, wary. Up close, his eyes were startlingly blue. "It's a shame you're still celibate!" she said.

Her daring earned her the full weight of his attention.

Encouraged, Meg held out a carrot. "May I cook you dinner tonight before the show?"

The actor smiled again, pulled on a pair of expensive Italian sunglasses, reached out, covered Meg's left breast with his hand, pushed against it once, said, "No," and left.

Rude! Meg thought. The men she had met here were rude! Not kind, not courteous, rude! She wiped her eyes, which had filled with hurt, and closed her coat. I should count my blessings I never met Him here, she told herself. Ireland—it was raining again—was a dreary country full of dreary people. She ducked her head and hurried back through the downpour, hugging her groceries.

She was more upset than she meant to be and that night for the first time she got drunk. She went to one pub with her housemates, left them to go to another with a boy in a torn sweater, left him to go to another where she met the dour long-legged Professor Shaughnessy, whom she gaily addressed as Doctor Speed Freak, and with whom she shared her innermost thoughts about the Celtic Tiger (meow), the Celtic Theater (zzzz) and the Celtic Cuisine (crisps beat cabbage hands down—she said that four or five times while slapping her hands palm down on the table). When he excused himself and did not come back she accepted an offer to dance from a Yugoslavian waiter and sometime around three in the morning she ended up with the boy in the torn sweater again. They went into an alley, she lifted her skirt, he entered, she felt the first sweet shock of contact and then nothing except the bruise forming on her coccyx as it bumped against the bricks and the pain in her ovary. "Mind yourself, now," the boy said as he zipped up. "Thank you," Meg said and went home.

There were hugs and promises from her housemates as they left the next day and A's and gratuitous "brilliants" on all her papers. At Shannon, Meg, red hair growing out, gray roots showing, green contacts stowed in their case and bifocals back in place over her bloodshot brown eyes, gave The Fates a final chance to take over, but no charming stranger approached her in any of the endless lines and her seatmates were nuns. She did notice the same sleek flight attendant going through his same self-satisfied paces, and when he came around for drinks, bending over her in unconvincing solicitude, she kept her eyes on her magazine. Just before landing, she unbuckled her seatbelt to use the lavatory, but when she stood the pain in her ovary kicked in so powerfully it brought her to her knees in the aisle. The last thing she saw were the flight attendant's hands, small, white, and far better manicured than her own, stretched out to catch her.

One of his hands was in hers when she came to, and he stayed with her as the plane landed and she was whisked off for an emergency hysterectomy. His name was Frank Flanagan, he was Irish-American, he had been in the priesthood in his twenties, left it, married, his wife had run off with another woman, he was raising a teenage daughter alone, he had noticed Meg a month ago, the way she took care of that little boy, he had thought about her, how lovely she was, and all he could say was it must have been God's will that had finally brought them together. His breath was bad, his teeth were false, he had been in treatment for alcoholism six times and he talked constantly, smoothing his hair and glancing at himself in every reflective surface, but Meg felt the life in his soft polished hands and held on. She would say yes when he asked her to marry him. She would be happy. She would make him happy. And all of her friends would dance at their wedding.

Just Looking

Women in their fifties shop. There is nothing they need anymore but there is still one thing they want, one final perfect thing they have never found that might just have arrived, might be gone if they wait. They come first thing in the morning, leave last thing at night; they come with dyed hair and gray roots, toned biceps, slack bellies, smudged reading glasses, rundown running shoes. They flush with a slight, welcome, criminal rush as they push through the front doors. For they are not supposed to be here. They know that. They are supposed to be at home with their tired husbands, grown children, aging parents, incontinent pets. They are supposed to be at work, screening patients, arguing cases, toting columns of figures, correcting student essays. Instead, purses pressed to their sides, eyes darting, steps quick, they enter the bright glassy maze of the mall.

Once inside, they stay. Hours pass as they slip through the aisles, rise and fall on the escalators, circle the fountains, fishponds, and flowerpots blocking their way. Their nostrils flatten, flare, flatten again as they follow a trail only they know, a faint siren scent that leads through the smog of potpourri, the exciting dead whiffs of new perfumes, the stench of sweet grease from the food courts. Starving, they do not stop to eat. Parched, they do not drink. The bottles of water they brought lie forgotten on the floors of the cars they slammed into parking places they have also forgotten. They finger labels, hold crystal goblets to the light, press beaded earrings to their lobes, turn their heads from side to side. They test exercise equipment, submit to makeovers, read the back covers of novels, flick through racks of CDs. They try on clothes they will never wear and clothes they have worn ten, twenty, thirty years before. They take no pleasure in putting these clothes on or taking them off, yet put them on and take them off they do, averting their eyes from their fallen flesh in the mirror, half wanting to fall themselves to the pin-littered carpet and rest.

They cannot rest. Even though the fluorescent lights, the gossip of clerks, the rumble of carts, the scrape of zippers and the dull pulse of programmed music hurt their heads, they cannot fall. They know what would happen if they did: they would never get up, and other women in their fifties would step right over them, headed toward the china, the bath salts, the luggage, the snow boots.

And that mustn't happen. The women push back the dressing room curtains, step out, and continue their zigzag, stop and start, off and on search.

There is still time, they tell themselves. Time to find *it* before time runs out, time to want *it* before they no longer know what wanting is.

Sifting through silks at a table, parting a rack of reduced sequined gowns, checking the price of a watch exactly like the one on their own weary wrists, they lift their heads to the question they have heard all day, all night, whatever it is, wherever they are. *May I Help You?* the questioner asks. Sometimes a young face, sometimes a face like their own, tired, strained, anxious eyes elsewhere. *No. Oh no*, the women say. They rub their stiff necks. *Looking*, they explain, their voices brave as they smile and move on. *Just looking*.

Eskimo Diet

Dad said if I didn't lose weight he was not going to take me to the Ball. He'd take someone else. Some scullery girl, or one of the footmen's sisters. He'd say she was his daughter. He'd give her dancing lessons, buy her a red dress and let her wear the rubies. He might even let her keep the rubies. Of course, he said, he would rather take me, his real daughter, instead of spending all that money on a total stranger. But, Dad sighed, look at you. Princess, stop eating for a second and look at you.

I put down my fork, picked up the mirror, rubbed the grease off it with my sleeve, and looked. I saw what I usually saw. No big deal.

You're fat, Dad said. You could live off your own fat for a year, he said, like an Eskimo. He rose to go. At the door to my tower he turned and pointed his finger. Lose weight, he commanded. I don't care how you do it. But do it. The lock clicked behind him.

I sat on by the barred window and thought about Eskimos. I knew they chewed blubber. But that was whale blubber. Did they chew their own blubber too? How? I unlaced my bodice and examined my belly. It reminded me of pudding with a few little raisins sprinkled here and there. It looked delicious. But no way was I cutting into it. There must be another way. I felt something stuck between my teeth and tongued out a meaty morsel that looked good as new; a second banquet was probably stowed in my back molars alone. My arms and shoulders were red from stretching them out through the bars toward the sunshine and I saw that my sunburn was starting to peel. The peel looked like thin sugar crisps. I pulled off a small strip and put it in my mouth. Yum. Not sugary, not salty, sort of tangy, with a chewy elastic texture I hadn't expected. I probably had enough peel for one meal, maybe more.

So that's how it started. First I just ate floss finds and peel. I found if I tugged my sunburn too hard, little drops of rich coppery tomato-y blood bubbled out. I lapped as much of it as I could out of the places I could reach and when my period came a few days later, well, what can I say, it was payday in a bucket. Dandruff turned out to be bland as ricotta cheese but fingernail shards added texture. Tooth tartar was another white food but I thought oh well what can it hurt and scraped it up anyway. Toffee-tasting earwax made a decent dessert. I had long since stopped bribing my guards for treats. I *was* a treat! My nose alone was a cornucopia of goodies, a veritable soda fountain, bakery, and butcher shop all in one. It gave me thick milk shakes first thing in the morning and then as the day went on and my phlegm crisped up, little protein-packed nuggets appeared, sometimes with clear noodles of mucus that slipped down my throat sweet as fresh oysters. Scabs were chewy, toe jam gooey. Pimples, popped, yielded globs of thick cream sprinkled with blackheads tiny as poppy seeds. My vagina, I discovered, packed a rich yellow curd and I could either lick it off my forefinger warm and unsalted, straight from the source, or take it salted with one or two drops of fresh tears. I drank plenty of pee for hydration, of course, and though at first

I hesitated to eat my own excrement I found that formed into patties and grilled in the hearth it was really no worse than unicorn chops, and greased on both sides with underarm sweat and served with a little blood ketchup and a few skin peel crisps it was actually pretty good.

Needless to say, I was losing weight like mad and when Dad came back to check on me the week before the Ball he was blown away. At last, he said, I have a daughter I can be proud of. He threw open the tower doors and led me downstairs to the dressmakers and hairdressers and shoemakers and when I was finally gowned in royal red and covered in rubies we went off to the Ball. I met the Prince that night and the rest is happily-ever-after, except I did pay the storytellers to leave out the part where the Prince and I put Dad on the ice floe. "It's what the Eskimos do," we explained as we gave the floe a hearty push out to sea and waved goodbye.

Married to the Mop

The divorce was Lori's idea and it was a bad one. It had taken her all summer to convince her husband that they should separate, but once she did, he moved fast; he bought a red Corvette, moved to a penthouse in the city, and started dating an exquisite Chinese woman fifteen years his junior. This left Lori free to marry Stuart. But Stuart, who had begged her to marry him, suddenly cooled and broke up with her in an email. Lori found herself alone in the suburbs with two teenaged sons, a cancer-riddled dog, a pregnant cat, an ancient Subaru, a falling-down house, and nothing in the bank. Christmas was coming. She would have to get a job.

Lori had once worked at a riding stable, but she had quit after her second pregnancy, and she didn't know anyone, anymore, who still needed a blacksmith. She was too hostile to be a salesgirl, too undisciplined to be a personal trainer, too restless to work in an office, and too scattered to serve drinks or wait tables. Sitting in the bathtub with a bottle of red wine one night she began to weep as she tried to figure out how she was going to cover the bad check she had just written to the veterinarian for the dog's first chemo treatment.

Married to the Mop

It was while trying to scrub the circle of red Chianti off the white enamel rim of the tub that Lori got the idea: she could clean houses. She would not have to dress, no one would care about her swollen eyes and stringy hair, the physical exercise would be good for her, and she could arrange her hours so she would be home before the boys returned from school. The boys, of course, were not to know. No one was to know. After all, there was something shameful about cleaning other people's houses.

She posted an ad under an assumed name and began work right away. Her first client was a silent woman in a muumuu who pointed out two of the biggest wall ovens Lori had ever seen, one set above the other, with a broiler beneath. All three were black caves hung with thick, stiff, greasy stalactites. Lori gamely donned her rubber gloves and reached for the oven spray she had brought with her but the woman touched her nose and coughed, and Lori understood she was allergic and that this was to be a chemical-free zone. She would have to clean the ovens with nothing but hot water and a sponge. It took four hours, with the woman sitting beside her the whole time, reading a spiritual help book by the Dalai Lama, and at the end, Lori was paid only half of what she had asked for.

The next client asked her to clean a children's playroom. This was easy, work Lori was used to, and she felt almost cheerful as she picked up and sorted Transformer parts, loose beads, crayons, hair ornaments, and Legos; she crawled under a bookcase to retrieve a diaper filled with feces, tottered on a chair to bat a deflated balloon down from the ceiling, carted out fossilized food finds, shook out shag rugs, hung up tutus and Spiderman costumes. She had the place immaculate by the time the children came home and she watched in amazement as in two seconds flat they demolished it. "Well this was a waste of time," their mother observed, and Lori again had to pocket less than she'd asked for. She saw another client that same afternoon, an old man who followed her around as she vacuumed his apartment, touching her hips with his light old hand. Her final client that week was a single woman her age, with a glassy condo overlooking the lake, a refrigerator full of champagne, steak, and chocolate, and two closets full of designer clothes—and that job of course, despite the easy work and full pay, was the hardest.

They were all hard. Not because of the work. Because of the people. Lori liked creating calm out of chaos but she was not used to being treated like a servant. Because of her dark hair and olive skin she was often assumed to be Hispanic. She was spoken to either in loud English or execrable Spanish, which, out of pride, she sometimes corrected under her breath. She had, after all, lived outside Madrid studying equine management for two years before her marriage; she had led horse tours through the Pyrenees. She was careful to keep her head down when she spoke and not spit in annoyance when she was asked to enter and leave through a side door, to wear a cap and apron, to use the guest latrine.

Word got around about her excellent work and her clientele grew. Soon she had one or two jobs every day. Her hands were ruined, but she had never been vain about her hands, and she was able to pay for the vet and to buy her sons the racing bikes they wanted for Christmas. She even made a friend, a young Guatemalan gardener named Ephraim, who worked some of the same houses she did, and who made her laugh as she joined him for lunch in the front seat of his truck.

It was Ephraim who gave her the idea. He wasn't stealing, exactly, he explained, just taking a plant here, a sapling there, a few cuttings, some extra tools, bags of mulch that would not be missed. He was planning, he told her, to go into business with his brothers soon; they were going to open their own nursery.

He never, he told her, wide-eyed, lying, took from the clients he liked. Only from those he did not like.

Lori didn't like any of her clients, but still, like Ephraim, she knew to start small. She took little things that would annoy: a single jigsaw piece from a puzzle, a library book, the vegetable peeler. When the old man she cleaned for reached for her hip she calmly pivoted, held out her hand and demanded fifty dollars, which he promptly paid that week and every week thereafter. She began to feel more at home in the homes she felt least welcome in. She helped herself to fancy foods she found in the refrigerators, ate them bouncing gently on king-size beds while watching television, pirated medicine cabinets, dabbed expensive perfumes behind her ears, opened drawers, entered closets, tried on dresses, shoes, furs, wigs. She loosened light bulbs, reset alarm clocks, dismantled remote controls, reprogrammed computers, rinsed toothbrushes out in the toilet. She was going a little crazy, she knew, but at least she had gained some weight, was drinking less, sleeping better, and no longer wept in the bathtub.

She might have continued like this indefinitely but one morning her ad was answered by Stuart—the same Stuart who had begged her to leave her husband and marry him. Stuart wanted someone to prep his house while he and his young bride-to-be were out tasting wedding cakes. His fiancée had not yet seen his house, he wrote, and he wanted everything to look perfect.

Perfect? Lori wrote back, using her assumed name. *I can do perfect.* She drove up to his house on the appointed day, found the key where he'd left it under the mat, and got to work. It only took a few hours to exchange his Viagra for some powerful emetics, replace the photos on his mantel with ones of naked men, tuck a dead crab firmly and irretrievably into his heating vent, place pretty vases of poison oak and rag weed on the night stands, break the zippers on all his suit pants, tap into a child porn site on his computer with an alert to the police, and hang a pair of sheer thong panties on his exercise bike. As a final touch, she folded the toilet paper into an origami heart before she left.

Of course, Stuart would know who had done it (they were, after all, her panties), and as Lori sat with the five new kittens on her lap and the dog at her feet the next morning, she realized that she was going to have to find another line of work. As if to agree, the dog started to whimper, reminding her of his appointment at the vet's that day. The animal hospital waiting room was, as always, a mess, and Lori automatically began to tidy it as she waited, arranging the magazines, wiping fingerprints off the glass aquarium, straightening the heartworm and tick posters on the walls, and sweeping up the loose tufts of animal hair on the floor. When the vet returned to tell her the chemo had been successful and her damn dog would live a little longer, he looked around with approval. "I need an assistant," he said. "Interested?" He held out his hand. It had been so long since anyone had held out a hand in simple democratic friendship that at first Lori didn't know what to do with it. And if the vet noticed anything in her palm when she finally roused herself to shake back he was too polite to mention it and anyway the next day at work Lori dropped the tiny ceramic castle back into the aquarium, holding her breath as it wobbled, then settled upright on the clean bright sand.

Seahorse Sex

At first she sees nothing but worms in water. But as her sight adjusts to the darkened aquarium, the woman sees that each seahorse is unique. Some are saddled with stripes, some are crowned with wreaths, some have tiny dragon wings. Each moves in its own way, speeding, or rocking, or gently idling. She follows a red one, a green one, a swift orange courser. One pair seems to be mated. Freckled in gray and brown batik, they rise together, slide sideways through the long green grasses together, descend to the coarse sand floor to sway back and forth in place like Javanese dancers. They have proud ridged manes, outthrust chests, long articulated tails, gold sequin eyes.

She smiles, thinking of her husband. She remembers that seahorses are loyal and mate for life, that the male even carries the babies.

A docent sidles up as she peers into the tank. "See how small their mouths are?" he says in his retired salesman's voice. Yes; she sees; their mouths are tiny yellow suction cups at the end of a fairy's long trumpet. "They can only eat what will fit into their mouths," he confides, "and," his voice lowers in disgust, "they eat all the time."

Seahorse Sex

The woman is relieved when he leaves. She does not want him to see what she now wants to watch.

For her two are about to have sex.

The larger one passes over the smaller one. He pauses, returns, brushes over her again while she waits, submissive, the eyelash fins at her neck and flank fluttering. When he descends, she dips her head. He winds his tail around hers, seeking her center with his tip. The woman holds her breath as both lift their necks in unison. Just then another seahorse, a slim young gilded thing, slips out of nowhere, dances toward them, pirouettes around the male, brushes him with her pretty tail, and then—unbelievably—draws him toward her.

The woman leans forward and raps the glass with her wedding ring. All three seahorses separate and rise to different sides of the tank, indifferent, inviolate, upright, acting as if nothing has happened, as, of course, nothing has.

The docent, beside her in the dark, chuckles.

The woman spins away. Back on the cold city streets, her cell phone pressed to her ear, she listens as it rings, unanswered, again and again.

Banyan

Jane flexed her neck, rotated her shoulders, and looked up from her guidebook as the plane dropped through the clouds to the Big Island. She could see Mac and Mia, four rows ahead of her, Mia's tousled head turned toward the window, Mac's long legs stretched out on the aisle, both still asleep. How did they do it? Jane could never sleep when she traveled, too much to take in, too much to think about, but her lover and her daughter had crossed their arms and closed their eyes the minute the plane left Seattle five hours ago. They were going to miss their first glimpse of the volcano! She pried a macadamia nut from its package, aimed at Mac's neck and watched him start, rub the spot where it hit, then lean over and touch Mia's face to wake her for landing.

The old lady beside Jane snorted and Jane waited, expecting the snort to turn into one of the nasty low laughs she had been subjected to throughout the trip, but her seatmate only pointed to the open guidebook. "Romantic Hawaii!" the chapter heading gushed, "The perfect place for your dream wedding!"

Jane, shamed, snapped the book shut. She did not want her fantasies, mundane as they were (Mac proposing to her over mai tais, Mia radiant with approval) mocked, especially by this crazy witch. She was used to lunatics seeking her out and sitting beside her—she had some sort of unholy radar that pulled them right in—and this creature, decked out in stained sweats and hiking boots, carrying an ancient shih tzu in a bamboo cricket cage, had focused on her at once, settling down with a rush of incoherent mutterings. Her long white hair had a burnt electric stench and the long nails on her wrinkled brown hands were filthy. She had refused to move when Jane needed the restroom and when Jane, forced to step over her, had tripped, she had chuckled. During Jane's absence, she had drained Jane's gin and tonic. Her dog, a horror of bristles, whiskers, snot and drool, had growled at Jane the entire trip and now, as the plane taxied into the Kona airport, began to snap toothlessly at her from its cage. Jane let her own lip curl back, then rose with relief as the seatbelt lights went off. She gathered her things and made her way down the aisle.

Mac and Mia were already out the exit door and Mia, on the tarmac, was already bent over, clutching her midriff while Mac, helpless, patted her back with his big hand. Jane quickened her steps to catch up to them.

"The wounded bird act," Jane explained.

Mia moaned musically, almost, if you weren't used to it, Jane thought, convincingly.

"She always does this," Jane explained, looking into Mac's worried face. "She's thirteen years old and this is how she travels. What is it, honey?" she asked Mia.

"I have a temperature," Mia said.

Jane pressed a hand to Mia's forehead. It was damp, fresh, cool as a petal. She bent and kissed it, feeling Mia's startled retreat. "You're fine." She looked up to see Mia's pretty pout reflected in Mac's new aviator sunglasses—huge, expensive, ridiculous glasses—why on earth had he bought them? At forty-five, Mac was still a good-looking man, tall and broad shouldered. There had been no need for him to dye his hair, bleach his teeth, and yellow his skin with self-tanner for this trip. He looked like a gigolo. Of course there had been no need for her to get Botox injections, scarlet lip gloss, and a new cropped haircut either. No wonder Mia feels sick, Jane thought; she probably doesn't want to be seen in public with either one of us.

"Are you sure she doesn't need a doctor?" Mac asked.

"Positive. Smell the air!" Jane added brightly. "All I could smell on the plane was dog farts and old lady. But Hawaii smells like flowers."

It did. Flowers and coconut oil, ripe fruit and salt air. Alone at the carousel, Jane reclaimed their luggage, raised her head, and smiled up at a misty rainbow over the airport. She watched Mac drift over to a lei stand, choose a spray of plumeria, and drape it over Mia's bent neck. It was just like Mac, a land-scape architect, to go to the flowers first, and she smiled, then winced as Mia, consistently bad mannered, hunched her shoulders, hugged her elbows, stared at the ground, and sneezed. It seemed Mia had given up on Lyme Disease, mono, multiple sclerosis and leprosy for this trip at least, and had settled on a simple cold. Good, Jane thought. She could deal with a cold.

"You said it would be hot here," Mia complained. "I'm freezing!"

"I'm on fire," Jane countered. And her face, glimpsed in the window of the rental car as she slid inside, did look flushed and puffy, her hair spiked in damp strands, her nose shiny. An unwelcome shaft of heat shot through her as she slammed the door shut and tugged wrinkled silk off her sweaty chest and thighs.

"You all right, sweetie?" Mac, turning to back the car out, patted Mia's knee. "You need an aspirin or anything?"

"I can't take aspirin." Mia moved her knee aside and opened another of the enormous vampire novels she had been reading all summer.

"She chokes. Oh look!" Jane pointed to a second rainbow arcing across the sky.

The ocean glistened gray on one side and jagged mountains rose green on the other. The island was less lush than the guide-book had promised and had an arid clarity she had not expect-ed. As they pulled onto the highway she saw the old woman with the dog. She was wearing a sequined visor and sunglasses and her long brown thumb was crooked out to hitchhike.

"Don't stop!" Jane warned, but Mac was hitting the radio buttons to find a station Mia liked and didn't even look up. Jane slid down in her seat as they passed. When she raised up, the woman was far behind and the road had opened onto a moon-scape of lava rocks with messages and hearts outlined on them in white coral. *U N I 4-EVAH*, Jane read aloud. She reached over to press Mac's hand. He pressed back and she relaxed. Things had been strained lately, with her heavy caseload at the law firm and his recent lay-off, but they would be lovers again, she knew, once they were alone.

But they were not to be alone. When they got to Kona, they found there had been a mix-up and only one room was reserved for them. A holistic health conference had taken over the entire hotel and this was the last room available, the manager told them. "We'll go to another hotel," Jane decided.

"I can't afford another hotel," Mac reminded her. Jane dropped her eyes. The flight, the food, the rental car were all her treat. She had wanted to pay for their lodging too—the trip had been her idea and she made more money than Mac—but Mac had insisted. It was, he had said, the least he could do. It was also, Jane knew, all he could do.

Banyan

"The room is big." The manager, a large, honey-colored Hawaiian woman, stretched her arms wide. "You'll like it. Two beds. Family style."

"No family I ever," Jane began, but Mac took the keys and Jane and Mia followed him up the elevator to an airy room overlooking the roofs of other hotels and the ocean beyond. The two queen-sized beds were within hand-holding distance and as Jane shook her head, Mia, sneezing dryly, threw her things down on one of them, rummaged through her duffel bag, and locked herself in the bathroom.

"It's fine," Mac said. "We'll take it."

"But we won't be able to make love!" Jane could not keep the disappointment out of her voice.

"We'll just have to be inventive. Mia will be down at the pool, won't she, or out at the beach? Every teenage boy on the island will be offering to teach her to surf."

"Mia won't surf."

"You'd be surprised what she might do once she gets the chance. I might even teach her myself," Mac said.

"I thought you were going to teach me."

"You too, if you want."

He turned on the huge television, preset to a video about the island's volcano.

"Kilauea's still erupting," he whistled. "Look at that." His bleached teeth shone unevenly below his dyed mustache as he whistled again, and Jane, following his gaze, saw Mia emerge from the bathroom in her new bikini. "You look dangerous, sweetie," Mac said, and Mia, with a filthy look toward Jane, sneezed again.

"You going to join us, Mom? We'll be down at the pool." Mac held his arm out to Mia, who stepped forward lightly.

"No. 'Mom' is going to stay here by herself," Jane snapped, "and watch TV all afternoon."

Banyan

No one heard her. Mac's pleased voice faded as he led Mia down the hall. Alone in the hotel room, Jane opened her suitcase and threw her new lace lingerie into the back of a drawer. She reached to turn the television off, but the image of Kilauea caught her. It looked exactly like a black heart with red blood pouring out. She picked up Mia's discarded lei, sniffed it— why hadn't Mac bought her one too?—dropped it, and began to pace, her own heart beating faster and faster. She knew why Mac hadn't bought her a lei, hadn't sat with her on the plane, hadn't noticed her new haircut. In the last few weeks, Mac had changed. He had changed toward her and he had changed toward Mia. He had always treated Mia with amused indifference—his girlfriend's spoiled kid—but recently he had offered to help Mia with homework, had picked her up from dance class, taken her side in disputes over dishes and laundry. He had remembered her birthday with a pair of tickets to a rock concert, seemed almost comically disappointed when she invited a friend and not him, and had forgotten Jane's birthday altogether. His cheerful bedtime complaints about his bad back, bad knees, and leg cramps had sanitized their sex life and he had been "too tired" to even celebrate their two-year anniversary last month.

A familiar yip sounded from the hotel corridor and Jane froze as the shih tzu shot past the open door. Was that evil hag following her? Wasn't this supposed to be the "big" island? She slammed the door shut with the flat of her hand, leaned against it, then sank to the floor, pressing her face to her knees. She'd read *Lolita*. She'd seen both versions of the movie. As an attorney, she'd defended child victims and she'd prosecuted child molesters. Nothing like that was going to happen here. She would just have to be careful. Very very careful. She put on her own bikini, turned off the television, and joined the others at the pool.

They went swimming, sunbathed, walked along the sea wall. As night fell, they sat on a green bench near an enormous banyan tree, watching Japanese tourists take pictures of themselves and listening to the clamor of the nesting birds above. "This tree," Jane remembered from her guidebook, "came from India hundreds of years ago. They call it the strangle tree because it can't stop growing. It sends out so many roots it ends up strangling itself."

"Dark and shady back in there," Mac said. "Looks like a good place to hide from the island police and smoke a little *pahalo*."

Jane stared at him. Had he lost his mind? *Pahalo?* Mac never smoked marijuana, and he loved trees. The first time she had seen him he had been arguing with construction workers who were planning to take down an old oak outside her law office. But now he only smiled at Mia, tugged his dyed mustache, and didn't give the huge tree another glance. Mia, leaning against Jane's shoulder, sniffled piteously, swung her slim legs and didn't look either.

When the streetlights came on, they continued to stroll, cruising the art galleries with their airbrushed blue whales and smiley dolphins, the gift shops with their koa wood bowls and plastic grass skirts. They ended up in a New Age crystal shop. While Mia examined the soaps and lotions and Mac fooled with a "native" drum, Jane studied her charges.

Mac was trying to show Mia how fast he could drum. Mia's indifference was heart's ease to observe, but that was because Mac was too new at this to know how to seduce her; you don't rope children in with things that interest you, Jane thought, you go after children with things that interest them. She watched his sad blink as Mia moved away. It would do no good to accuse him of being in love with her daughter; he'd be shocked; he'd deny it; he'd say she was crazy. And Mia would be equally horrified. Mac, she'd protest, was old enough to be her father, the father she hadn't seen since she was six, the father who never wrote or sent gifts—why would she want someone like him?

Someone snickered behind her and Jane swung around to see an old woman pass through the doorway. Setting down the tray of dyed shells from the Philippines she'd been sifting through, she watched until the woman disappeared in the crowd.

That night Jane lay awake listening to the surf, the trade winds, the call of the doves. Lonesome, she rolled over to kiss Mac, but he inched away, his body cool beneath the sheets. After an hour, she slipped out of bed, went to the desk, turned on a small light, and finished reading the guidebook. She had already learned the history of the islands—all that trickery, cruelty and corruption—so tonight she read the legends. She read about the miniature Menehune and their fish ponds, and about Maui, the boy who caught the sun with a fishhook. Finally she read about Pele, goddess of the volcano. Whenever anything annoyed her, Pele blew up. She didn't listen to excuses, apologies, or promises; she never held a trial, prosecuted a criminal or defended a victim; she simply erupted, efficient and brutal, and lava'd everyone to death. You had to respect a temper like that, Jane decided, closing the book. Pele might have ended up alone, but she ended up satisfied.

She looked over at the two sleepers. Mac's arm was stretched toward Mia's bed and Mia's round brown shoulder was exposed. As she pulled Mia's sheet up, Jane saw a scrap of faded cotton quilt—Mia had secretly packed her old blankie, the blankie Jane had made for her when she was a baby. Jane smiled and bent to kiss Mia goodnight. As she inhaled the familiar drugstore odors of watermelon and strawberry in her daughter's hair, she smelled something else, bright and new, a sour trace of womanly sweat. She dropped the sheet and slipped back into her own bed, moving Mac as far over to the wall as she could.

Banyan

The next morning Mac suggested they go snorkeling. It would be "a serious experience"—when had he started to talk this way?—and Mia would see all sorts of "outrageous" reef fish—she might even see a barracuda. Jane marveled again at his innocence as Mia predictably said, "No way." They drove to a black sand beach and Mia spread a towel out, plopped down, and closed her eyes, her box of unused tissues beside her. Jane picked up the huge book Mia had been reading. "Valdred parted the silken bed curtains and growled with blood lust at the sight of Delphia's pulsing purity." No wonder Mia felt sick, with garbage like that in her head. When had she stopped reading *Little House on the Prairie*? While Jane was off trying molestation cases? Trying to make enough money to pay their mortgage and buy their groceries?

She put the book down and sat hugging her knees. A solitary woman in a rusty black one-piece bathing suit stood waist-deep in the water, pulling a mask on over her face. Jane remembered snorkeling years ago with college friends, the fun it had been, and after a while she picked up her own mask and snorkel and followed the other swimmer into the ocean.

It was still fun. The shallows flickered with bright butterfly fish, wrasse, and parrotfish, and the sound of her own breathing through the tube was intimate and encouraging. At first she stayed in the shallows, but something sweet, slow, and shadowy drew her deeper and she saw to her delight that she was only inches from a large sea turtle, his mild eyes and mossy beak guiding her silently through a boulder garden studded with corals. Hidden underwater, she relaxed her vigilance. How safe and peaceful it was down here! She swept soundlessly into the warm currents, her hands opening wide to wing her forward. Silver bubbles broke as the woman in the black suit splashed ahead, leading her out deeper and deeper. I could stay down here forever, Jane thought, and the desire to do just that startled her so that she surfaced with a kick and struck for shore. She was just in time to see Mac on his knees looming over Mia's bare back, tenderly applying sun block. Neither looked up as Jane dripped toward them. At the other end of the beach, the woman in the black suit emerged from the surf and pulled off her mask, releasing a cloud of white hair as she snatched up a small dog and crabbed off toward the parking lot.

"Pele's here," Jane said.

"Someone you know?" Mac asked.

Jane stared after the woman, then squatted down on her towel and groped through her bag for the guidebook. "Pele," she read out loud, "vengeful goddess of the volcano, often appears in the guise of an old woman with a white dog. She can often be seen hitchhiking along the highway. She lives deep inside the Kilauea Crater and accepts offerings at its rim; she is said to be particularly fond of cigarettes and gin."

Mia turned her head, eyes closed. "What's she vengeful about?" Mia asked.

"Her lover was a pig god," Jane explained. "And one day, when Pele was visiting another island, he seduced her younger sister."

Mia made a pretty face and arched her back. "Yick. Pig god."

"Oh, they're not a bad sort." Mac capped the sun block lotion. "Once you get to know them."

"She roasted him on a spit, served him at a luau, turned her sister into a pineapple, and had her canned," Jane improvised.

"Right. And you just saw her."

"I see her all the time. She's everywhere."

Everywhere was intolerable and every day got worse. They went to the City of Refuge, where early Hawaiians had fled to escape the wrath of their kings, and Mac said wouldn't it be nice to live in a place like that, outside the law, where you could do anything you liked, with whomever you wanted. They went to a sacred altar at the tip of the island where King Kamehameha had been born, and as Jane frowned at the rough carved birthing stone, Mac picked flowers for Mia's backpack. They drove to the Pololu Valley Lookout and while Jane photographed the view, Mac photographed Mia.

On and on it went. Mac wooed Mia and Mia sniffled and read her book and Jane was sad and mad and hurt and could not show it because—what was the point? What could she do? If she spelled out the obvious she would ruin everyone's vacation; if she simply sat on her feelings she would only ruin her own. On the next to last night, after a romantic sunset dinner at the guidebook's favorite restaurant, where, instead of asking Jane to marry him, Mac raised his mai tai and said, "To Mia's first time in Hawaii, may there be many more," Jane pleaded a headache and walked off by herself. Mia wasn't in danger. Mac would never rape her. He loved her too much to harm her. Jane had never had anyone love her that much. Had anyone ever loved her at all? Mia's father, for a while. Mia herself, for a while.

Wearily, drearily, Jane drifted through crowds of tourists and locals, stopping at a grocery store for a bottle of gin, not even minding that the old woman who sold it to her had white hair and an ancient Jack Russell asleep on a straw mat. When she passed the huge banyan tree, she ducked and went in.

It was a hideous tree, with its dangling gray vines and ridged roots intersecting in haphazard connections. It was dim and musty inside and seemed wild with invisible bird life. Jane sat down, drank straight from the bottle, and looked up at the crazy web over her head. It seemed that anything that wanted to could grow here, in any direction. It was like Hawaii itself, she decided, with its easy philosophy of acceptance. Under this tree, everything was possible, everything was permitted. A middle-aged man in love with a thirteen-year-old girl? No problem. A jealous mother hallucinating goddesses? Welcome.

Everyone was welcome here. For a while. And then the tree gave out, gave up, had to, died. It could only accept so much, because so much was unacceptable.

On their last day they went to the crater. They had already gone to see the lava spill at the sea, the thin streams of red pouring over the black rock, the dramatic puffs of steam as fire hit the waves. But Kilauea itself, Mac said, was something to save for the end. Things worth having, he said, were worth waiting for. He gave a brave false wink to Jane as he said this, as if willing her to think he was referring to sex, sex with her, which had not happened all week and would probably never happen again. "You seem distant," he said, glancing at her as he drove. She nodded without answering. They had entered the rainforest at the base of the volcano. Yellow ginger and royal purple princess plants tumbled over each other in jungle profusion, crowding out the older native foliage around them. Mac turned the radio up—rap music—and said over his shoulder to Mia, "Do you dig this, sweetie?" but Mia, in the back seat, had her headphones on. She hadn't said anything except the usual, "I don't feel good," since breakfast.

"I don't dig it," Jane said. "If you care what I dig."

"Of course I do." Mac clicked the radio off. They curved up the Crater Rim Road and started through the lava fields. It was a new landscape up here, totally different from the flowering green jungles below, a high vast plain of pewter-colored rubble pocked with cracks and crevices of smoke. Jane watched a frigate bird soar through the warm gray air over the lifeless plateau and took in a shallow sniff of sulfur, then another, its dark eggy odor weighting her lungs. Her throat felt crowded with short hot bad words; her eyes burned; her pulse twitched. When they came to the end of the road, she turned to Mia.

"Want to come see where Pele lives?"

"I can see it from here." Mia turned a page of her book.

"Mac?"

"I'll stay with Mia."

"Not if I can help it." Jane heard her voice break and saw her face reflected in Mac's sunglasses. This tense, tight-lipped woman was his girlfriend? No wonder he preferred the daughter. Who wouldn't? She got out alone, slammed the door, and started up the path.

The air smelled of sewage and the loose lava tinkled like glass beneath her feet as she climbed to the top. Offerings to the goddess crusted the rim of the crater: seashells, coins wrapped in ti leaves, cigarettes, dried leis. She crouched to set her own offerings down: the half-empty bottle of gin, the guidebook. She straightened and stared into the great smoky hollow, which was, as she knew it would be, empty. An empty socket that stared blindly back at all who stared blindly in. Nothing there. Never had been. It was tempting to give a great roar and spread her arms and jump in, incinerating with rage as she dropped to the bottom. Tempting too to turn aside and hold on to this rage, to let it smolder as she grew older and angrier and more and more bitter. She glanced over her shoulder at the rental car in the parking lot. Mia's pale face shone in the back seat and Mac was a large shadow slumped over the steering wheel. They looked alone, unconnected, and almost—she hesitated— asleep? She could see Mia's hands folded against her cheek, pressed to the window, Mac's big shoulders rising and falling in rhythmic slumber.

Is it possible, Jane thought, that I've been the only one awake this whole trip? She waited, braced for a breath of rude laughter. But the crater was silent. She started back toward the car and got in. "We were worried about you, Mom," Mia said, stretching, "you were gone so long." Mac nodded, yawned, and started the engine. Silently, they drove down the long loop of the gray mountain road. As they took the last curve, they passed an old woman bouncing in the back of a pickup truck driven by two bare-chested island boys. Her baseball cap was askew on her wiry white hair, her muumuu billowed, her dog barked from her lap, and her eyes glowed like hot coals. She grinned straight at Jane with her toothless mouth and waved. Jane, turning to watch her recede, saw a thin flow of lava begin to pour from the pierced heart of the mountain. By the time they reached town it had diminished to a simple line of moonlight and when they flew home the next morning it was nothing but haze on the ocean. Still, Jane knew it was there. She would always know it was there.

Straw Man

Recently, instead of just walking into a room, Robert has started to think: "*He* walked into a room." This kind of thinking is new for him and Robert doesn't like it. What does it mean? Does it mean he is turning into a writer? His mother was a writer and he hopes to God he is not like her. She would have written, "*I* walked into a room." All Meme's stories were about herself; she never wrote about anyone else. And those rooms she wrote herself walking into? God. Bedrooms. Always bedrooms. Bedrooms of people she should never have slept with, other people's husbands, her parole officers, Robert's best friend in high school, for Christ's sake. The night that Robert heard her with Torre, he threw his gym clothes into a paper bag, slammed out the front door, and biked across town to move in with his swim coach.

His brothers should have left then too, maybe that would have saved them, but they stayed. Jay is dead now and Charlie might as well be dead, sleeping on the streets in LA somewhere. The stepfathers are dead, Uncle Ricky is dead, Torre is dead. So that leaves Robert. The survivor. The one with the college degree, the steady job, the wife, the twins, the swimming pool, the bird feeder, the two-car garage.

Meme survived too, of course, for a while at least. After that last rehab she joined AA, fell in love with two of her sponsors, married one of them, took up yoga, studied astronomy, taught ESL in night school and continued to write. It took a long time for the emphysema, heart disease, diabetes and cirrhosis to get her and when it did it was Robert who nursed her, paid off her debts, buried her, and brought home her damn cats. And then what? Suddenly, out of nowhere, a New York editor "discovers" Meme's old stories and Meme becomes famous. Her book is on the bestseller list right now, there is talk it may be nominated for a Pulitzer Prize. It has already been translated into fourteen languages. Fourteen!

Which means that in fourteen different languages people know that Robert's father was a schizophrenic and Jay's father was a heroin addict and Charlie's father was married to Uncle Ricky's mother and Uncle Ricky had AIDS and Grandma was a psychopath and Grandpa was an embezzler. Meme didn't leave anything out. See page 98 for how Uncle Ricky hung himself. See page 99 for how Robert found him. See page 117 for Robert wetting his bed, see page 230 for Robert caught shoplifting. Meme didn't even change his name! Sometimes she assigned deeds to him one of his brothers had done; sometimes she got their names mixed up; he has had to read every story in the book carefully, sometimes twice, looking for himself. Not everything is recorded. Torre's motorcycle accident is missing, and Jay's death, choking on vomit, that's gone. But Meme being pushed to the edge of the roof with a knife at her throat at that crack house in Goleta, her affair with the court psychiatrist—those "stories" she kept, those are in the book.

Why did she have to tell everyone everything? What made her do it? Sitting at the kitchen table between shifts at the diner with the Jim Beam beside her, typing on the IBM she got from a pawn shop. Or scribbling at the welfare office with a spiral notebook on her knee. Or crouched in the front seat of her car, waiting for some cop to come up and ticket her, penciling words onto the blank back of a utility bill. She published the stories here, there, little magazines, literary magazines that no one read, none of Robert's friends anyway; he'd deny she was his mother if they asked. He wasn't proud of her; he never bragged about her. Why would he? She embarrassed him. She betrayed him and yet now that her stories have been collected all the reviewers are saying, How brave. How true. What a heroine.

Heroine? Meme was an alcoholic. She had the shakes every morning. She couldn't put on lipstick without smearing it half over her face. Her breath reeked. She had hairy arms; sometimes she singed the hairs off with a match and the kitchen stank for hours after. Her periods went on for weeks. She wore torn hose with sandals. Snorted so hard when she laughed snot shot out. Cried so hard when she cried more snot shot out. Stole table tips from other waitresses, stole library books by the armful. Bummed cigarettes from bums, dealt drugs with dealers. She killed Torre with her crazy love for him, she killed Uncle Ricky with her crazy hate for him, she tried to kill herself with a bottle of Tylenol. Tylenol! That's who Meme was.

If Robert is in fact turning into a writer, he should set the record straight, write about his mother from the perspective of someone who truly knew her. Not one of the besotted reviewers, not one of her new foreign fans. But how? His brothers had talent—Jay's one-act play won scholarships to colleges he never made it to and Charlie's rap songs rang through the metro. Like Meme, his brothers spun gold from the straw of their lives. Robert has actual gold—he earns a six-figure salary and will take his family to Europe next year—but when he writes his words die on the page.

And that's okay. That's for the best. Meme's book money keeps rolling in, one royalty check after another, all of which Robert banks for Charlie, if Charlie ever shows up. He doesn't want a cent for himself. He wants nothing of Meme's, he wants to put her behind him. And yet. He keeps seeing their old kitchen in their old apartment where Meme used to sit, tap tap tapping on those typewriter keys. He smells her perfume and hears the inhale, exhale of her cigarette, hears her murmur a word or two under her breath as she types, sees her swivel on her chair, turn to him, blank eyed at first, then suddenly breaking into that warm, loving, lipstick-smeared smile, so glad to see him. She holds out her arms.

And someone wants to walk through the door. Not Robert. *Him.* The other one. The mouth-breather, the bed-wetter, the bad loser, the skinny kid who studied, who stuttered, who *prayed.* And that kid can't speak up for himself. He doesn't, as Meme joked when she explained why she never used the rope she kept looped over the garage rafters, have the hang of it. All *he* wants to do is crawl into Meme's lap and pet her and protect her and put his hands around her throat and squeeze the living shit out of her and how can anyone write about that?

Ears

The first thing Cal said when he saw the baby was "Thank God she's got my ears"—an innocent observation, no harm intended, and in fact Cal did have handsome ears, small and rosy and pointy and as flat against his head as two pressed palms—but Petra didn't like hearing that and struggled up in her hospital bed to tell him so. "I never knew you didn't like my ears," she said. Cal didn't answer. He wasn't listening. Handsome as his ears were, they were often attuned to things other than his wife's voice and right now he was more interested in his daughter's tiny breaths, the beat of a baseball game from a television down the hall, and the rumblings of his stomach (he hadn't eaten since Petra had gone into labor the night before). He continued to beam down at their baby. "So all this time you've hated my ears," Petra continued, "and you've admired your own. I never guessed that you thought your ears were better than mine. You are vainer than I suspected, Cal. Colder." Cal looked up, eyes glowing. "She's beautiful," he said, of the baby. "I thought you thought I was beautiful," Petra said, or should have said right then and there to get it over with. She leaned back against the pillows, the birth blood still pooling hot between her legs.

Ears

"I thought you thought I was the love of your life. But now I see I was wrong. I've been replaced. You love that baby more than you love me and you love her because she reminds you of you. That's pure narcissism, Cal. You should be ashamed." Cal was not ashamed then, but over the remaining years of their marriage he became ashamed, and confused, and, of course, increasingly deaf, and by the end of their marriage he was silent as well. The baby bloomed into womanhood and one day Petra glanced over at her daughter, astonished by the perfection of her ears. "They are exactly like your father's," she began but the daughter had heard enough in her lifetime and covered them both with two pressed palms.

Paradise

Claire wasn't dressed for the rain and it blind-sided her, literally, as she'd forgotten her glasses as well as her jacket. She ducked her head and hurried across campus, trying not to bump into lampposts or trees. It was clear from the deserted quad that she'd be late for class once again, and once again the other students would snicker, the professor would sigh, The Young Republican would smirk. *Pansies*, her father's voice said. *They're jealous*, her mother chimed in. *You're more talented than all of them*, Dr. Carmine soothed. *Just don't get a swell head*, her father chuckled.

I won't, Claire promised, clattering up the stairs to the third floor of the Fine Arts Building. She stopped on the last landing to catch her breath and laugh. How could she get a "swell head"? She was a forty-two-year-old unemployed barista. She had no money. Her son was in jail. Her lover had dumped her. She unwound the black chiffon scarf with the silver stars that she'd bought once in Paris and wrung it out, then, head high, she slipped into the Life Drawing studio with her brightest smile. Every class had to have its clown. "Sorry," she said, going to the sink for some paper towels to rub through her wet hair.

"What was it this time?" the professor asked but before Claire could answer, "Injured possum?" he suggested. "Phone call from a telemarketer whose wife just left him? Mormon missionary starved for a home cooked meal?"—all excuses Claire had given in the past, but they were real excuses, she never made anything up. Hurt, she met the professor's studied twinkle.

It seemed wrong that someone so hard and smug should be teaching something as soft and vulnerable as the naked human body.

"I was visiting my son in jail," she explained but the professor only laughed as if that was funny and nodded toward the empty dais. "I'm canceling class anyway," the professor said. "Our model couldn't come."

"Can't someone else model?" Claire turned and held out her hands to the redhead with the Japanese tattoos, the bald guy with the hairy chest, the fat girl with the broken nose. Silence. *Shame on them,* her mother tutted. *Pussies,* her father agreed. *Go for it,* Dr. Carmine suggested. Claire raised her chin. "I'll sit." She twisted her wet hair into a knot on top of her head. "I used to model all the time." That was a lie but honestly how hard could it be? "And besides," she added, remembering, "I forgot my glasses so I can't draw today anyway. Oh but I did remember to bring my assignment." She slipped off her backpack and pulled out the sketch she'd done from the photograph of her parents taken two days before their plane went down. They were at a coffee plantation in Uganda, passing out medical supplies and grinning like teenagers, surrounded by laughing children. "I had trouble with the perspective," she lied, hoping to make the other students feel better about their own drawings, but the professor barely glanced at her work before setting it down on a workbench. *Prick,* her dad offered. *I think he's in love with you,* her mother whispered.

"Miss Stelanski has volunteered to sit for us today," the professor drawled. "That all right with everyone?" There was silence except from The Young Republican, who said, "Thanks, Miss Stelanski," which was nice of him and totally unexpected although, come to think of it, conservatives did have better manners than liberals.

Happy to be of service, Claire slipped behind the alcove, kicked off her high heels and unzipped her party dress. She'd worn it hoping to cheer her son up but nothing she did cheered Finn up anymore; he'd spent the whole visit with his back to her and his hands over his ears. *All sixteen-year-olds are like that,* from her ever-faithful chorus, but even her mother's voice sounded uncertain. Finn's parole officer had been flat out rude about her plans for home schooling, and just kept repeating that Finn "was a danger to himself and others"—which was a fancy way of saying he had threatened the arresting officer with his skateboard. A skateboard against a police revolver? *Pig*, hissed her father. *That cop is the one who should be in jail*, huffed her mother. *Clearly a paranoid personality*, agreed Dr. Carmine.

Claire hung her dress up, examined her face in the little mirror, dabbed some more kohl on her eyes, rouged her cheeks, ran her fingers through her pubic hair to fluff it, and went to the couch. "Sitting or standing?" she asked the professor as the students circled their easels around her.

"You choose," the professor said, not looking at her.

Reclining, Claire decided. She was tired. This couch was not as nice as the one she used to curl up on in Dr. Carmine's cozy office; it was scratchy and the springs poked her ribs, but after she got over her nervousness and stopped grinning at everyone, she was able to relax. Things had been so stressful lately she'd forgotten the art of being still. She used to be good at it. *You still are!* Yes, she agreed, but she couldn't keep her thoughts from Finn. Was he really, as the parole officer said, "hypomanic"? What did that even mean? Dr. Carmine started to explain but Claire's parents shushed her. *It's a dumb word*, Dr. Carmine conceded. Claire nodded and stared out at the cypress trees in the courtyard whipping around in the rain. Rain was the excuse her lover had given for not coming last Sunday—a lot better reason than the one she heard The Young Republican giving the professor right now.

"I work all week," he was saying, "The only free time I have is Sunday afternoons and I can't concentrate on my assignments then because that's when this crazy nymphomaniac upstairs has sex with her boyfriend. Everyone in the building can hear her. We've all called the super but once she starts in..."

Claire moved her eyes without turning her head. "What building?"

"The Grenville."

"That's me," Claire explained. Everyone in the class stopped drawing and she couldn't help it, she broke the pose and laughed out loud, a belly laugh that brought snot to her nose. This was too funny. "I thought I saw you in the stairwell once," she said to The Young Republican. "When did you move in?"

"Last month," he answered, hushed.

"Yes, well, I'm sorry to inform you that my 'boyfriend' as you call him didn't come last Sunday because he stayed home with his wife so it's not my fault you didn't do your homework, sorry again, I didn't mean to put you on the spot. What do you think of our super by the way? He's the reason my son's in jail, if it weren't for Mr. Onorato calling the cops Finn would be home safe right this minute and not sitting in a cell sharing a pit toilet with a bunch of highly disturbed gang members..."

Claire, her father warned. *TMI*, her mother whispered. *Why not?* Dr. Carmine argued, *it's true.*

Claire reached for a tissue and blew her nose.

"Class dismissed," the professor sighed.

She apologized again after she wiped her face and pulled on her red dress, which was still damp. "I shouldn't have said that about last Sunday," she said, wrapping her scarf around her neck. "I'm sorry." She peered over the Young Republican's shoulder at the sketch he had made. She saw a hag with crossed eyes and great tits. "Do you have a girlfriend?"

"Yes," The Young Republican said shortly, gathering his pencils.

"Well if you ever want someone to talk to, you know where to find me!"

He didn't answer. The professor cleared his throat behind her. "I suppose you need a ride home?" he said.

"With you?" Claire blurted. "No thanks! I got my car back from the impound yard last week," she explained, and then, embarrassed—he was just being nice!—said, "Maybe another time?"

It was still raining and as always it took forever to find her car and then to find her car keys and then to rip the drenched parking ticket off the windshield. She liked to take the coast highway home but today even the seagulls winging over the surf made her sad, plain old down-home sad. The Young Republican had been wrong to call her a nymphomaniac—she had only slept with twenty men her entire life and she had been in love with most of them—but he'd been right to draw her looking hideous. She was a mess. *You have your art*, her mother reminded her. *And your health*, her father chimed in. *Fake it 'til you make it*, Dr. Carmine advised.

I will, Claire nodded, and straightened up. Squinting, she drove through the rain, but even going slowly, she did not see the man step into the street in front of her, though she felt the thud as he hit the bumper. "Don't be dead!" she shouted. *He won't be!* everyone shouted back. Shaking, she braked and got out and knelt in the street beside him. The man was filthy, in oily jeans and a brown leather jacket, but his face as he lay on the cement was unmarked and his eyes when he opened them were green as canned peas. "Have I died?" he asked. "Have I gone to Paradise?"

"No," said Claire, not knowing where to begin to pat for broken bones.

"Are you an angel?"

"Are you hurt? Can you stand?"

"You look like an angel."

"It's the scarf. It has stars."

The man groped for his cap, a colorful number with tassels, like the ones Finn used to wear when he was a little boy, clapped it over his rust-colored curls, and got to his feet. He did not seem to be injured or bleeding, yet Claire could not stop trembling as she guided him out of the rain and into her car. The passenger seat was littered with old CDs and overdue art books from the library and she pushed them onto the floor to make room. The man settled in. The smell of him, earth, rain, and sewage, filled the car. His canvas shoes were torn at the seams. He wore no socks.

He's homeless, Claire thought. Now what? Emergency room? Church? Shelter? Mental hospital?

Don't catastrophize, warned Dr. Carmine. *You'll figure it out*, said her father. *He's got nice eyes*, said her mother.

"Where can I take you?" she asked the man, worried.

"Oh," the man said, "It's all right. I like it right here."

"Here?" Claire peered through the windshield past the overflowing dumpsters on the seawall to the long flat gray expanse of blowing sand, the breakers spitting in the cold wind. She shivered. Finn had liked this part of the city too. He had come down here at night when he couldn't sleep. "Ever see a sixteen-year-old boy skateboarding down the middle of the road?" she asked. "In the middle of the night?"

"Crazy kids," the man said cheerfully. He sounded like her father, saying that. "I hate to keep harping on this," he added, "get it? harping? But you are breathtakingly beautiful. Are you sure you're not an angel?"

Flattered, she couldn't help it, Claire bit back a surprised rush of tears. No one had called her breathtakingly beautiful in years. "I talk to angels," she confessed.

The man studied her. He did have nice eyes. "What do you talk about?"

"Oh." She paused. Not since Dr. Carmine's heart attack had she told anyone her secret. "I tell them my problems."

"And what do they say?"

"They say not to worry."

"Sounds good."

"It is."

"Well, better get a move on." He ducked his head and opened the door to leave. A swell of rain blew in.

"Wait!" Claire didn't know what she was going to say; she only knew it was dark out there. It was cold. It was wet. She thought of her tiny apartment—its odors of coffee and incense and turpentine, its bright paintings and worn rugs, her lover's last roses, dying in a vase, Finn's guitar and locked bedroom door... "Come to my place. I have a couch. You can take a hot shower. I'll heat up some soup." The man hesitated. "I have wine."

The man closed the door and turned to her, his broken teeth gleaming in the dark as he smiled. What am I doing? Claire thought as she turned the key. Am I doing the right thing?

You always do the right thing, her angels chimed.

Rinse. Swish. Spit

Raina's father left nothing but a bad smell. There was a man with no boundaries. Named all his kids after himself. Can you believe it? Raina was the oldest so she got slapped with Josephine. First thing she did when she left home at sixteen was go to a lawyer, lie about her age, and get her name changed; best money she ever spent too. Oh-oh, that hurts? Where? Here? And here too? Huh. One of Raina's three sisters, the crazy one, well, the craziest one, changed her name to Jubie. She meant to spell Julie but she got it wrong. Poor Jub gets everything wrong. She says O that movie was so scary it made the hairs on the back of my legs stand up! She says her husband went down on his hands and knees when he proposed! She is slightly to the right of Genghis Khan. As long as they don't talk about politics Raina adores her three sisters; they have a blast; laugh? They even go on cruises together. No cruises this year, though, no more trekking to Nepal or dive trips to Zanzibar because she and Rob are remodeling their house; you wouldn't believe the fights; her menopause is wearing him out, poor guy. You've heard how many menopausal women it takes to change a light bulb? Who the f—k cares? Raina doesn't get hot flashes like other women, she gets cold flashes; honestly, she's a corpse in bed; the other night when she got under the covers and tried to cuddle Rob yelled, "It's the Yeti" and she laughed so hard because he was sound asleep and the next morning she went online and ordered two abominable snowman costumes for Halloween. Last Halloween she and Rob went trick-or-treating around the neighborhood as the Jenners—she was Bruce and he was Caitlyn. You have to laugh. What other therapy is there? And speaking of therapists—you okay? It's a lot of buildup back here—Raina's last therapist turned out to be one of those full-body huggers you just feel sorry for, plus he called *her* seductive, and then said that was a compliment, oh right, so now she's seeing a woman. Men don't know what compliments are, do they. Raina's father's idea of a compliment was take your pants down. Raina saw her father at her uncle's funeral, first time she'd seen him in thirty years. He was sitting in a back pew all alone because no one would speak to him, well why should they, but Raina said You know what? I'm going to go talk to him and her sisters said Don't but she went up to him anyway and said Hello Joseph and he said Do I know you and she said I am your oldest daughter do you remember what you did to me as a child? And he thought and then he said I am sorry for what I did to you as a child and Raina said I forgive you and he nodded but she wasn't sure he understood because he spent the next fifteen minutes talking about himself, which is what he always did, you could not get a word in edgewise with that man, he never shut up and he never let anyone else talk, ever. You think it's bad having my hand in your mouth right now but how would you like to be six years old and have your father's dick in your mouth? Not good. Not good at all. Well, what can you expect. Total sociopath. He should have been sent to jail. Raina's trainer wept when she told him about forgiving her father but there's no point weeping; you have to make your own happiness, if you didn't have a happy childhood when you were a child you have to make a happy childhood for yourself when you're an adult. Right? Raina was a little old lady when she was six years old and even then she knew she never wanted to have children herself. That's why she loves playing with her nieces so much, she takes them on picnics and camping trips and sends them out on scavenger hunts. Now of course they all want to live with her but Raina assures them that would be the end of her reputation as The Best Auntie In The World because she would be tougher than their parents ever thought of being; she'd send them to Catholic school in the morning and military school in the afternoon and home school the hell out of them the rest of the time; they'd beg for mercy! Jubie and the unknown language, Korean or Dutch, but what else could she be saying but *something to drink* so she asked for an orange juice, astonished when the attendant unsmilingly handed her an actual orange. Well. Okay. She liked oranges. She began peeling the rind off only to find that it was a grapefruit dyed to look like an orange—why would anyone do that? She did not like grapefruit and dropped it into the vomit bag, flinching when she heard a splash. Someone began kicking her seat but when she turned she saw the entire row behind her was empty. And all the rows stretching to the back of the plane—empty as well? And on both sides? But wasn't this plane overbooked? Hadn't the desk clerk at the airport practically begged her to forfeit her ticket for cash and take a later flight? And she'd almost done so, too, almost decided to take him up on it, but when he'd dropped to his knees and pressed his lips to her knuckles, she'd been repelled and said No, she couldn't change her plans at the last minute and when he'd looked up and sneered *What plans?* she'd snatched her hands back and marched into line. Should she have said Yes? Had she made another mistake? She'd made so many mistakes in her travels! What was there about traveling that made her every assumption incorrect? "Assume," she remembered reading somewhere, "the word that makes an ass of you and me." She glanced out the window, crying out as a wedge of swans slammed past, then dropped her eyes to the aisle which was teeming with kittens in leather harnesses, pacing back and forth as intently as panthers. She drew her feet up to avoid getting bitten, then plugged her earphones in, crying out again as what sounded like seven trumpets blasted into her head. Tearing the plugs out she groped through her purse for a tissue, but her purse was gutted, nothing in it. She snapped it shut and bit back tears. Her fault. It had to be her fault. She must have left her purse open in a public place (but what public place?) and someone (who?) had helped himself to everything she owned (what had she owned?) which meant that a stranger now had her name and her address and her money and knew all her secrets. What were her secrets? Couldn't she at least be allowed to keep her own damn secrets?! It wasn't fair. It wasn't right. She plucked at the seatbelt which had begun to tighten around her, impatient to free herself. Why couldn't she live in the world the way others did, others who knew how to get from A to B, who knew how to ask questions and understand the answers? She swallowed hard as the plane began to lurch and buck and when the overhead bins burst open she covered her head with her arms. Bits of detritus banged against her, filthy surgical socks, sequined vests, scribbled apologies, ripped pajamas. She batted everything back and sat up straight. She could hear the engines whining down, the wheels beginning to drop, and even though looking down she saw only a crowded highway with people in cars staring straight up in terror she knew that once they landed she'd be able to focus, she'd be able to think, she'd be able to figure all of this out.

The Lawn Fairy

For the first year after James died, Ruth woke every morning with a bright sense of expectation. Surely today something good would happen. She would hear from James—there would be a message hidden in the house or arriving in the mail or left on her cell phone—a message of love. She had read that spirits only returned to tell the living that one thing: that they were still loved. James had died too quickly to tell her anything; an impatient man, he was gone by the time she got to the hospital and in any event he had never been effusive. He had never called her darling or princess or sweetheart; his birthday, anniversary, and Christmas gifts to her had always been practical—a piece of new kitchen equipment, a car. He ignored Valentine's Day. And yet Ruth had always felt sheltered and treasured in the rough thrust of his outflung arm in sleep, had found connection in the way his eyes sought hers at a party he wanted to leave. When he leaned back in his leather chair in the evening, eyes closed, earphones on, listening to his Verdi or his Mozart, she knew he needed her there, sitting across the room, reading, to complete his pleasure. She had been important to him. She could not stop thinking that she still was important to him, and that, any day now, he was going to let her know how much.

The house they had lived in together for the last thirty years was in need of repair and, partly to please James, Ruth began to remodel. She had the roof fixed, replaced the rain gutters, hired a contractor to refinish the scuffed wooden floors and put new double-glazed windows in the dining room. She painted the foyer a soft Tuscan gold, tore down the old drapes and replaced them with Roman blinds that opened up to the garden.

The garden, she saw with pleasure, was still doing well. She could take care of the shrubs and the roses; she always had. But the lawn! James had mowed the lawn with a fervor reserved only for his weekly squash games; he had taken great pride in it and it had always been immaculate. But now? Ruth bit her lip. He would be annoyed by the raggedy job she'd been doing and the neighbor boy she had hired to take over had done no better. She would have to hire a professional.

She phoned around and settled on a service that promised to cut the lawn for forty dollars whenever it needed. She never saw the mower. She would come home from errands or a luncheon or a book club meeting and the lawn would be fresh, green, immaculate. There was never a bill. When she phoned the service to find out where she should send her check, she got only an answering machine. Not knowing how to pay, she began to slip two twenties under the doormat when she left in the morning and even if she returned an hour later, the money would be gone and the lawn would be perfect. This went on until autumn, when the afternoon rains stopped and the air was dry and the grass seemed content to stay the same length, though it was browning and crisp underfoot.

One night the doorbell rang. She put down her book and peered out. A short stout Hispanic man in a baseball cap stood on her porch. "Who are you?" she called through the door. "The mower," he answered.

Ah! She opened the door and was met with a brilliant flash of gold teeth. The mower's smile was so warm she smiled back. "I wasn't sure you existed," she confessed.

"Existed?" he repeated, as if the word puzzled him, and then, in perfect English, he asked if she was married. Surprised, Ruth said, "No."

"Divorced?"

"No," she said again. "I'm widowed. My husband died."

The mower's brown eyes filled with tears and then he took his cap off and tipped his head up to the sky; Ruth followed his gaze to the stars. "You will dance again," he said softly. Struck by the poetry of his promise, Ruth said, "Oh I hope so, yes, I long to," and suddenly she knew she would. She would dance again! She felt the mower take her hand. His touch was light and tender.

"Saturday night?" he asked.

Ruth leapt back and closed the door in his face. Her heart was pounding. The mower had asked her out? She paced the house, shaking as she double locked every door and window. She spent a fitful night on her side of the marriage bed, dreaming about the lawn. In her dream the grass was growing, getting taller and taller until it towered over the roses, and then it began to spread, carpeting the path, choking the bird bath, pressing against the windows of the house, threading its thick way up to the front door, blocking the door, trapping her. The dream was so real that for the first time since James's death she awoke in terror and pain. She ran downstairs to peer out the front. No one was on the porch. The door opened effortlessly. The lawn lay in even stubble before her, short and brown. All was fine. She'd been a fool to worry. But how quiet it was! There wasn't a car on the street, a child on the sidewalk, a single bird in the leafless trees. The morning sky was white and bright and vacant above her. She closed her eyes to shut it out and then it occurred to her: James had sent the mower. He must have.

Barefoot, she stepped onto the lawn and began looking for something, a dropped bouquet, a box of drugstore chocolates, some sign, anything.

Two Words

Roy got up at five to start cooking for the firemen. He had been getting up at dawn for weeks now anyway, ever since the last seizure, but usually he just read his affirmations and practiced Tai Chi in front of the turned-off television set. Today he wanted to talk. He couldn't wake Jill; she needed her sleep and, as their marriage counselor had pointed out, she also needed plain and simple "time out," because Roy (and Roy knew this, and was sorry) was driving her crazy. So Roy slipped out of bed and went to his daughter's room. Baby Tess lifted her arms and allowed herself to be carried to the kitchen but she squirmed and covered her ears with her blanket the minute he opened his mouth, so Roy had no choice but to address God as he understood Him.

Or Her. For Roy's God was a girl, about twelve years old, slim and lazy with lit dewy eyes and sharp little teeth. She could be generous and fond one minute and casually vicious the next. He had felt Her sour breath on his neck since his childhood but had only named her God and honored Her as such since the diagnosis of his brain tumor six months ago. By trial and error he had also discovered, at about the same time, that the best way to treat Her was with extravagant respect. No matter how badly She herself behaved, She expected good manners from him. She especially liked to be thanked.

Thank you God, he said silently, sitting naked on the kitchen floor among the tumbled cookbooks with his palms turned up and his closed eyelids jumping as fast as his pulse, *for all the people I've known who are up there with you now, including* (he counted) *mother, father, stepmother one, stepmother two, and Leslie, poor Leslie. May they be filled with lovingkindness. And in the meantime thank you for keeping me away from them and letting me live with these beloved strangers down here a while longer. Thank you for the Zen Center, the Positive Center, WellSpring, and Esalen. Thank you for chemo and radiation and antidepressants and aspirin and medical insurance. Thank you for all the doctors, even the last one.* He paused and passed one hand over his bald head, pleased as always by the plush resilience of skin over skull. *Thank you for giving me a nice round head. Thank you for making it the color of mozzarella.* Thinking of mozzarella made him remember the lasagna he had promised the firemen. *Thank you*, he finished, palms tingling, eyelids twitching, Baby Tess poking at the dragonfly tattoo on his thigh, *for helping me find the right recipe.*

He had spent the day before at the library, going through cookbooks. He had explained to the librarians that he wanted a recipe that was saucy and cheesy and rich, and it was astonishing to both him and the three helpful women how many so-called good cookbooks called for low-fat cottage cheese in place of ricotta, yogurt in place of white sauce, ground turkey or even sliced zucchini in place of sausage and beef. Some chefs used no salt; others relied on oregano only, and none gave directions for making the noodles from scratch. He had no luck finding the recipe he'd used as a boy, working alone in his father's bachelor apartment, but Martha Stewart, of all people, had a cookbook that offered a passable compromise and if he combined it with recipes from four other books, he knew he'd have a killer sauce, fit for heroes...

"Roy!" Jill said, coming into the kitchen. "What are you doing?" She stopped. The marriage counselor had told her not to assign blame. "Are you all right?" she asked, her voice intent on softening.

"I'm fine." Roy opened his eyes, flexed his palms, and smiled. He always smiled when he saw Jill. She was so pretty and young and quick. Her eyes matched the blue of her bathrobe, the blue of the ribbon around her long drooping ponytail. She was the best thing that had ever happened to him, he told her that all the time, and at first she used to chime in and say No, *you* are the best thing that has ever happened to *me*, but she didn't say that anymore. "I knew there would be problems," Jill had told the counselor last week? the week before? "I mean, he's ten years older and widowed and had a baby but I never thought there would be problems like this. I never imagined this."

Who could? First the trouble with his balance. Then the memory loops. Handwriting shot. Headaches like train wrecks. "And now," Jill had said, "I have two children. Two children and I've never even been pregnant!" She'd started to laugh but then she'd burst into tears and Roy had sunk into a ball, right there on the counselor's carpet, curled up, hugging her ankles, rocking back and forth, crying too, so sorry he'd done this to her, so sorry! Until at last she reached down and said, "It's all right." But it wasn't. It couldn't be. What had he cooked for poor Jill on their first date? Wild duck? Caviar risotto? The road to hell, Roy thought, is paved with food inventions.

Thinking of food made him jiggle Baby Tess off his thigh and hand her to Jill who cupped her up incompetently and stood there looking at him. Beauties, both of them. "I'm a lucky man," he said, as Jill carried Baby Tess back to her crib. He stood, waited until the dizziness sank and he was sure he was not going to keel over, then tied an apron over his bare belly, found his reading glasses by the phone and opened the cookbooks to all their marked places. Make the noodles first. Then the three sauces. Assemble. For dessert, good vanilla ice cream, fresh strawberries, and the same chocolate chip cookies he'd made for the boy after his first seizure, when he'd writhed in the rain in the middle of the street until the delivery van braked for him. He could still hear the boy's high, astonished voice. *You're fucking lucky to be alive, man. You're a miracle, man.* And he was. Nothing but a bruised hip from that one. And other miracles followed. A dislocated shoulder from a fall in the shower had been fixed with one good whack from the chiropractor. A tumble off the roof that should have broken his neck only banged up one knee. Jill had yanked his arm back in time from the garbage disposal. God had screamed "Truck!" in his ear the last day he'd driven. He'd swerved off the road and though he'd cut his eyebrow on the steering wheel there was no mark now. Odd the parts of the body that decided to heal, while the tumor wavered, shrinking and then swelling again, capricious. Five years, one doctor said. Five minutes, the last one had said.

He shook out his morning dose of deadly meds, swallowed them down with Willard's Water, and began to measure out flour for the pasta. After a while, excited by the elasticity of the dough beneath his hands as he kneaded, he forgot his promise to be quiet if he got up early, opened his mouth, and started to sing.

Jill heard him but she wasn't mad. She smiled when she came back in to make coffee, a slight smile, not granting much, but enough to let him know that the sight of a bald man dressed in nothing but an apron, draping noodles to dry over the backs of kitchen chairs while singing "You Are The Sunshine Of My Life" was all right, was fine, was funny, was sweet. She had not smiled at all last month, was it last month? month before? when he'd risen at dawn to rearrange the living room—she had not liked the Feng Shui; he'd had to put everything back. She'd been upset when he'd cut the plum tree down—it almost fell on the house—and after he'd pulled the carpet up to expose the genuine, if battered, parquet underneath, she'd forbidden him to refinish the floors. But since the last seizure, on the hiking trail, she'd been gentler. And now, as she opened the refrigerator for milk and saw the packages of ground beef and Italian sausage he'd forgotten to add to the tomato sauce, she was almost as upset for him as he was for himself.

"I want the firemen to like this," Roy explained, fighting tears as he sautéed more garlic and added the meat. He leaned over the flaming pan and tried to kiss Jill on the cheek. She gasped and reached for the handle in time. "I want them to like you," he added, chastised, moving back as she waved him toward a chair. "I want one of them to like you a lot."

"You're not making sense," Jill sighed. She said that often.

But she was wrong.

"You can't really be mad at him." He heard her on the phone later that day as he was painting Baby Tess's toenails. She'd wanted blue. "It's the medication he's on. They change it every week. They don't know what they're doing." He blew on Baby Tess's toes until they were dry, then fit one fat foot into a new red sandal.

"Ready to walk to the store?" he asked.

"No," Baby Tess said. "Park."

"Okay, we'll walk to the park."

"No," Baby Tess said. "Store."

He looked into her fierce eyes. "You are just like your mother," he revealed. Baby Tess, who had never known Leslie and thought Jill was her mother, raised a fist and he kissed it.

"I'll say one thing about those firemen." Jill paused. He could actually hear her lick her lips across the length of the room. "Eye candy. Total eye candy."

Good, Roy thought. He smiled as he fit the second sandal onto Baby Tess's foot. So Jill had noticed after all. He just hoped she'd noticed the right one. Two of the firemen had given him CPR, two others had carried him down the trail on a stretcher, but it was the tall strong one who had stayed with him in the ambulance, soothing Jill in a deep voice, that he was counting on. Stu. The chief. Roy pulled on his beret and followed Baby Tess to the front door. "Bye, love," he called. "We're going to the store." Baby Tess opened her mouth to scream. "Park," he amended. "I'll be back in time to make the cookies." Jill, on the phone, giggled throatily, ignoring him. Am I jealous? he wondered. He shut the door and trudged down the driveway. He hoped he wasn't jealous. It was all right for Baby Tess to be like her, but he himself did not want to be like Leslie.

Leslie. His first wife. The one who had died. Leslie's last days had been so miserable that Roy had taken them to heart as life's lesson. No whining for him, no complaining, none of that Why Me—it just made things worse. Who knew why God dumped a bucket of bad luck on one person and slipped a promise ring onto the finger of another? It made no sense. Leslie had had a grotesque life. She'd been orphaned as a baby, abused as a child, abandoned as a teenager. He'd been thrilled by her nervy blonde looks and her easy articulate self-pity. He'd cooked—what had he cooked for Leslie on their wedding night?—rack of lamb in pomegranate sauce? And then, with no warning, she'd been stricken with a rapid, debilitating, and very rare form of MS. It was a joke; it was no joke. The pregnancy she refused to terminate was a horror; she was blind, crippled, furious. She blamed him; she blamed Baby Tess. She sat in the dark and begged for a gun, over and over, *just get me a gun, god damn you, do something right for once.* She'd probably be deeply gratified to see what had happened to him now. She'd probably say, *You see? I was right. No one escapes. Not even you, Mister People Pleaser. Mister How Can I Help You. Mister Totally Useless.*

He nodded to Mrs. Holst, who lived across the street, and stopped, Baby Tess yanking hard on his hand, to talk to Old Ed, the neighbor on the left, about the new stop sign. Was it a good thing? A bad thing? A good and a bad thing? Gypsy the Brogans' dog met them at the corner and was soon joined by Marcus, the Kleins' lab, and Flip, the Legaspis' mutt. "We are leading the dog parade," Roy said to Baby Tess. "They want to go to the park too."

"Store," Baby Tess corrected, but the minute he turned toward the store she steered him toward the park, where he happily spent the next hour, two hours? half hour? pushing her in the swing, throwing sticks for the dogs, digging in the sandbox for China. When he came home, the house smelled like chocolate—Jill had gone ahead and baked the cookies for him—and there was time for a bath and a nap before they drove to the firehouse. There was even time to paint his own toenails blue.

The firemen were waiting at the firehouse door, seven of them, maybe not "eye candy," but good-looking men nonetheless, better looking than Roy had been in his prime. Stu in his crisp white jacket introduced the others: Scott, Skip, Steve, Stan, Scott Again, and Sam. They ranged in age from twenty-one to about sixty, but they all had thick heads of hair, wide shoulders, and open outdoorsy faces. "I salute you," Roy said, shaking hands. "You are my heroes." Stu laughed politely; he probably heard that all the time, but a few of the other S's gave him strange looks. Roy knew what they saw: a puffed pale freak with wide lit eyes whose life they had saved once and might need to save again soon. Until then, a voter. A homeowner. Proud father of a cute, if clingy, little girl (Baby Tess was clamped around his neck) and a pretty, much younger, wife. Jill had washed her hair and released it from its ponytail so it waved over her shoulders. She was wearing rose perfume and slick brown lipstick. Two of the firemen helped Roy carry the foil-wrapped casseroles, the garlic bread, and the salad in from the car. Places were already set at a long table in front of an enormous television set. The baseball game was on and Jill asked intelligent questions about it. Roy did not care for baseball but he chuckled attentively as one of the Scotts reported on the inning they had just missed.

Stu gave them a tour of the station before dinner. Jill admired the new computer system while Roy studied the huge county map on the office wall. "This is where you found me," he said, pointing to a dotted hiking trail. "I won't let him walk there anymore," Jill chimed in, sounding authentically wifely. "Now I just go to the store and the park," Roy agreed. "Hospital," Baby Tess offered, lifting her head off his neck, her first words in an hour. "But we drive him to the hospital, honey," Jill explained to Baby Tess, "he doesn't walk there." "That would be a long walk," Stu said. Strong chin. Strong back. Ringless. Roy smiled and moved in.

"Jill is a wonderful woman, isn't she," he said, "beautiful, the best, and Baby Tess, what a darling. And you know what?" He looked up into Stu's clear hazel eyes. "They would be all alone now if you hadn't helped me."

"That's our job," the firemen said, all of them, one after the other, looking neither pleased nor puzzled, just matter of fact.

"Well it may be your job," Roy continued at dinner, "but I want to make a toast anyway." He stood and lifted his plastic glass of lemonade to the table. "I'm only sorry this isn't champagne," he began. "Or," amending that at the sight of the flat polite looks that met him, "beer." The men relaxed and smiled. He was glad to see they had all helped themselves heartily to lasagna and bread. "It's a crazy thing to bring dinner to the world's greatest cooks—everyone knows firemen are the world's greatest cooks—but I've been cooking since I was eleven—I used to cook for my father after he left my mother—that's how he got women, my father, and what a miserable lot he got, poor guy, he'd bring them back to the apartment and I'd cook for them—you might say my brisket cooked his goose—anyway, I know, honey—" to Jill—"I'll get to it, the thing is, I couldn't think how else to say thank you. I wouldn't be here tonight if it weren't for you guys. You saved my life and I just wanted you to know how grateful I am. That's it. That's all. Just thank you." He put down his glass and clapped and Jill and then, surprisingly, Baby Tess, clapped with him.

The firemen waited until Stu said, "Sure, no problem," and then they all ate and the conversation turned to jobs in general, Roy telling them how he thought his old job in sales was probably the reason he had the tumor in the first place, all that getting up and getting dressed and getting out every day when he never, not once, wanted to, and Stu, smiling at Jill, saying there wasn't a day when he didn't feel happy to go to work, and Jill saying she was lucky to be able to work at home now that Roy needed watching, and one of the S's saying he had once, years ago, thought of being a policeman instead of a fireman.

"Oh but that's a dirty job," another S said.

"The things you see," another agreed.

"Makes you hate human nature," another said. "Makes you mean."

"Policemen are mean," Roy agreed. "When my wife—my first wife, that is—died, a bunch of policemen came to the house. They..." he trailed away, stopped by Jill's curious look. He had never told her about Leslie's death. "They didn't come to help," he finished. He was glad when the S on his left asked about the lasagna recipe. The mention of Martha Stewart silenced everyone, then they recovered to talk of other entrepreneurs, stock tips, day trading, hobbies, sports, fishing, all interlaced with the shy references Roy had become used to about various bizarre illnesses and, as always when talking to other men, hairstyles. No one mentioned baldness, but it became clear from some clannish laughter at the end of the table that Stan used Grecian Formula and that Skip had a hairpiece. Stu could not bear to have his hair ruffled and Stan had a special comb no one else was allowed to touch.

"Is this what you do when there aren't any fires to put out?" Jill asked, sparkly. "Pick on each other?" The men laughed, blushed, hung their handsome heads. The casseroles and salads went around and around, followed by the cookies and ice cream and fruit. No one would let Roy clear, and although Jill tried to do the dishes, the men marched by her one by one and rinsed and loaded their own plates into the industrial-sized dishwasher. Roy crouched with Baby Tess by a white blackboard on the wall, helping her draw a wall of flames with colored chalk. He heard Jill from the kitchen talking to Stu in the same dramatic low voice she used at the marriage counselor's. How pretty she looked. How easy it would be. He'd simply invite Stu over to check the firebreak around the house next week. Leave an apricot pie on the counter to cool, make a pot of fresh coffee, and then take Baby Tess on a long walk; they'd go to the park and the store.

He straightened, tired. Jill saw his drained face and made their goodbyes and they left with their clean dishes, everyone waving. "Glad to see us go," Roy said, cheerful, as he sank into his seat in the car. "Now they can be themselves again."

"Oh I don't think so honey." Jill drove with both hands on top of the wheel. " I think they had a good time. That fire chief, Stu, told me hardly anyone ever thanks them. And that's a shame."

"It is," Roy agreed. He closed his eyes. His father had never thanked him for his stepmothers. Well, who would. Leslie had never thanked him either. "The thing we don't understand," the policemen kept saying, "is how she managed to kill herself with a gun in the first place. Blind and in a wheelchair? How'd she get a loaded gun?"

It would not have taken much on Leslie's part. She had time. He'd left pen and paper beside the revolver. A short note would have done it. Two words. But no. Forget it, Roy thought. It's over and done with. He felt God come down, heard Her hot little giggle, felt Her fingers, sharp and pointy, start to twist his skull as if it were the knob of a disliked doll. His head rose toward Her, light and obedient, a balloon in the night, ascending. Thank you, he forced himself to say. Thank you.

Sloane's Girl

Until the day of the faculty farewell, Mavis Trout was a beautiful woman. Even that day, mid-May of her sixty-fifth year, heads turned as she strode out of the auditorium and crossed the campus to the Composition Center. Her silver hair swung in a sleek pageboy and her hips swiveled like a girl's. With the help of two plastic surgeons, both of whom had propositioned her, she had retained the crazed kitten's face she'd been born with: small, sharply boned and freckled, with a bip of a nose and round, slightly crossed blue eyes that popped with intelligence and hostility. Her waist had thickened, her voice had thinned, and her mind had started to wander, but her mind had always wandered, that was its job, that was what made her such a good teacher. Who wanted a mind that stayed at home? Who wanted anything that stayed at home?

"Not I," said Mavis Trout, stalking up the stairs to her office. She ignored the girl waiting outside in the hall, plunged her key into the lock, kicked the door open, sank into the revolving chair behind her desk and turned toward the window, exposing a length of milky crinkled thigh beneath her slit black skirt.

The girl, Jenny Sanchez, hesitated. She had been to the farewell and had seen Dr. Trout drop the plaque at the Dean's feet. But her paper was finished, and it was late, and she needed it to get a grade. She took a deep breath, hunched her backpack off her shoulders, and entered.

"Welcome," Mavis said without turning around. "You have the great honor of being the last student I will ever see."

Jenny eased her backpack onto the weird fur couch Dr. Trout kept in the corner and unzipped it to look for her paper. "Thank you," she said. She shuffled through folders and textbooks, panicked. Where was her paper? What if she'd forgotten it this morning in her rush to get out of the apartment? What if it was still on the kitchen table? Or on the bus?

"Forced retirement," Mavis continued. "What a concept. Perfectly legal. Perfectly evil. Goodbye. Goodluck. And now get the hell out of here."

Jenny looked up, but Dr. Trout was not talking to her and when she looked down she saw her paper. It was stained where she'd spilled her coffee and wrinkled where the baby had grabbed it. She'd had trouble with the printer at the computer lab and some of the sentences were spaced on a slant. She smoothed the paper flat between both hands, the way her grandmother patted out tortillas. She was worried because Dr. Trout often gave students grades she'd made up: M for Messy or IBS for Illiterate Bull Shit. You had to petition Administration to get those grades changed before you could pass.

"So now what?" Mavis asked. "What should I do now with the rest of my life?"

Jenny shook her head, relieved, and offered the paper.

"I'm talking to you, dear. What should I do?"

Jenny dropped her eyes. Her paper was titled ESSAY NUMBER FOUR. The assignment had been to write an oral history from people you knew. She had interviewed Emilio and two of his brothers about being laid off at the garage. "Spend time with your family?" she suggested. Her voice came out squeaky. It was not the low calm voice she planned to use when she graduated and found work as a drug and alcohol counselor. "You will have time to be with your family," she said more firmly.

"I have no family."

"You have a husband," Jenny said, confused. "I saw him at the faculty farewell."

"Oh," Mavis said, sliding her silver bracelets up and down her thin arms. "Sloane."

"The writer."

"The hack," Mavis corrected her. "The gossip. The spy. The ancient betrayer."

Jenny frowned, uncertain. The old man had sat erect staring eagerly at Dr. Trout throughout the ceremony as if he was a deaf mute and she was his signer. Maybe he really was a deaf mute. One of Jenny's sister's boys had been born that way. But no, Dr. Trout had been the silent one. She had sat on the podium like a queen, her eyes the exact blue of the ribbon the Dean had draped over her neck and she had not said a word, not even when she dropped the plaque and walked out. Only the old man had broken the silence. "Isn't she wonderful?" he had cried, to no one, his voice high as a bird's. "Isn't she marvelous?"

"It looked like he loved you a lot," Jenny said boldly.

"How would you like to be stuck with someone who 'loved you a lot'?" Mavis asked. "Day in and day out."

Jenny, thinking of the baby left at daycare, shrugged and fixed her eyes on the photographs on the wall. They showed Dr. Trout in a low-cut black dress standing with a series of strange-looking men: a short curly-headed man in sunglasses, a tall hunch-shouldered man in a tweed jacket, a fat dark-eyed boy in fur. The men looked the same in every picture, proud and wet-lipped, and Dr. Trout looked the same too, sort of sexy and mad as hell. Jenny shivered. Mavis followed her eyes. "Poet. Novelist. Playwright. Sloane's famous subjects. Of course half of them are dead now. Most of them were dead before. This one," she tapped the man in the sunglasses, "couldn't keep it up and this one never came. Sloane loved hearing things like that. Of course Sloane has been impotent for years. Thank God."

Jenny nodded and held her paper out.

"So without this career," Mavis said, "if that's what it is, if teaching composition to incompetents for thirty years can be called a career, I am without resource. There is nothing else I can do. All I've ever known is the difference between *lie* and *lay* and *lying* and *getting laid*." She laughed, then her voice rose. "So you see my predicament. I'll be forced to look at Sloane, listen to Sloane, live with Sloane. Which is exactly what he's always wanted. Last night he said, and he didn't even care when I screamed, 'This is going to be like a second honeymoon.' Christ. Wasn't the first one bad enough? Do you know how long we've been married?"

Jenny opened her mouth, closed it.

"Forty-two years," Mavis said. "Do you know why we got married? Because I thought he could help me. Do you know why we stayed married? Because he could not. You of course do not understand that."

"No," Jenny agreed.

"Nor should you have to. It goes beyond the complexities of Comp 102."

Jenny nodded and glanced at her wristwatch. She had to catch the bus, get the baby, and meet Emilio at the courthouse in an hour. She looked up, startled to see Dr. Trout's popped eyes fixed on her navel. She reached to tug her tee shirt down.

"Where did you get that tattoo?" Mavis asked. "What is it? A spider?"

"Sunflower," Jenny said.

"Well give me your stupid little paper." Mavis took it, scrawled a huge A on top and handed it back.

"You're not even going to read it?"

"You were the only student who came to the faculty fare-well," Mavis explained.

"I thought we had to."

"You did? Well. That was a waste of your day wasn't it? Tell me," Mavis swiveled away toward the window again. "Have I taught you anything?"

"No," Jenny said, furious.

Mavis laughed. "I didn't think so. Well. Goodbye, dear. Good luck. Now get out."

Jenny grabbed her backpack and slammed out the door. Mavis heard her army boots drum down the hallway. Then, feeling like an actress, the way she had felt all her life in fact, she began to pack her books as she imagined an actress play-ing a professor packing her books for the last time would pack them. Showily, one by one, she picked up Sloane's bi-ographies, put on her reading glasses, and read the titles out loud in a mocking singsong: MIDDLE YEARS OF A MID-DLEWEIGHT, NAKED NARCISSUS, FIRST PERSON SINGULAR. She did not need to open the books to read the dedications: "To My Girl, Without Whom" etcetera. *Pimp*, she thought, as she'd always thought, the word plump and easy in her mind.

She turned and walked to the window. She could jump. She could throw the chair, the photos, and all the books out. But what good would that do. They were all replaceable. She herself was replaceable. No, she'd do what she'd meant to do. She'd give F's to everyone but the Sanchez girl and then she'd do what she'd never thought of before: she'd go to a tattoo parlor and get herself covered in spiders and come home and walk into

Sloane's bedroom as recklessly and wearily as she'd ever walked into the rooms of the others he'd sent her to, and she'd take off her clothes and pivot naked in front of him until he wept. Then she'd pack her suitcase and leave. It was time to retire.

Underage

Reno was Nat's idea.

"It's because you don't want a blood test," Terri guessed.

Nat did that cute thing with his mouth. He was terrified of doctors. Terri understood. She didn't like them either. Though she was half in love with the one she'd seen yesterday at the campus health center. "Take a semester off," Dr. Yamoto had advised. "Have the baby. Put it up for adoption. There's no stigma to that. This is 1960. Then come back to Berkeley and finish your sophomore year." Even as she promised she would, Terri knew she would not. She wasn't brave enough. "Nothing is as important as your education," Dr. Yamoto repeated and Terri dropped her eyes. There was no way she was going to tell this kind old man that she was getting a D minus minus in Physics, that her History TA had written "Nice try," on her blue book, that the entire Current Events class had sat in stony silence when, after a week of earnest reports on Sputnik, the Eichmann trial, and Red China, she had given her own presentation on "Will Liz Break Eddie's Heart?" The only class she was doing reasonably well in was English and that was because when

185

she read, she wasn't herself, she was Jude Fawley, she was Isabel Archer, she was in a safe place where no one could bother her.

If she had five hundred dollars she could go to Mexico. But she didn't have any money and none of her friends had any money, and anyway—abortion? It felt wrong. Nat agreed. He said not to worry, he'd do the right thing. He had been meaning to quit the team anyway, the coach was an idiot. All he asked was that Terri stop shoplifting and love the baby when it came.

Terri took the lit cigarette Nat handed her and stared into the woods. They were in Nat's Ranchero, parked at the end of a cul-de-sac, where they always parked. The accident had happened nine weeks ago. Warm night, warm whisky, stars overhead. She and Nat had broken up that night, and they had done it correctly for once: no tears, no accusations, they had simply hugged goodbye, and then, suddenly, Nat was inside her and then, suddenly, he had come, both of them surprised by how sweet and new it had felt, how—there was no other word for it—friendly.

They had not done it again. Terri thought Nat might have done it since with his old girlfriend Candy, but he said that hadn't happened, and she'd thought she might do it with the next boy who asked her but that hadn't happened either.

"We can drive up in a day and come back that night," Nat said, still talking about Reno. "They marry you right there in the courthouse."

"Okay," she said. "Let's go. Tonight."

"First we have to tell them."

"Why? Nat, I don't want to tell them. Please? Let's just get it over with."

"I need to ask your father's permission."

"You can ask for it after."

"Terri. If we're going to do this I want to do it right."

"He's going to be awful."

He was. They walked into the office hand in hand the next afternoon, and when her father looked up from his desk with a surprised smile, Nat manfully explained that they were "expecting" and would be eloping this weekend. Her father, no longer smiling, spun his chair around to consider Terri. "You have a stain on your blouse," he said.

Terri looked down. She should never wear white.

"When was the last time you combed your hair?" her father continued, his voice mild. "Or washed your face? Never mind. I'll phone your mother. Go on up to the house. I'll meet you there in twenty minutes."

"That wasn't bad," Nat said as they left.

Terry, thinking of her father's name for Nat, *The Jerk*, said nothing. "My mother is going to make this into one of her 'occasions,'" she warned as she and Nat drove toward her parents' house. "God damn hell shit."

"I hope you won't swear like this in front of the baby," Nat said.

"Little fucker," Terri murmured, but quietly, to herself. Who was this pushy little stranger butting into her body uninvited? She thought again of Dr. Yamoto, the courteous way he treated her, as if she mattered, as if she were an intelligent, ambitious, honest, cheerful and spirited college girl who had made one mistake but would get back on track and succeed in a career much like his own, not as a doctor perhaps but as some sort of important nurse, saving lives in third world countries. Well. Too late. She couldn't even save her own life, and she'd been far too cavalier about saving the life inside her. Last week she had tried sitting in a scalding bathtub and drinking a bottle of gin, which had worked in a movie she'd seen, but the minute the water burned her bottom she had hopped right out and poured the gin down the sink. A friend had volunteered to drive her up and down a rutted hillside in a borrowed MG with no springs, but they had stopped after fifteen minutes for milkshakes and French fries. She didn't have the heart to punch herself in the stomach and her constant silent entreaties to the creature inside her ("Just leave. Please. Go. Please Please Please Go") had clearly not taken effect.

What kind of mother am I going to be, she thought. Already the kid won't obey me.

Nat, seeing her smile, smiled back, relieved, and took her hand. "It's going to be all right," he said.

They said that a lot.

Her mother was sitting on a patio chair in her Bermuda shorts still holding a trowel and wearing a sun visor. She looked up, dry eyed. "Well," she said. "You got your man. Congratulations."

"What?"

Her mother shot her a quick hard woman-to-woman look that Terri didn't like. She thinks I planned this, Terri realized. She thinks this is what I want. She opened her mouth to explain but her mother shook her head and held up her hand.

"Someday you'll think about someone beside yourself," her mother said. She rose and held her arms out to Nat as he stepped onto the flagstones. "Nat," she cooed, "you handsome boy. Welcome to the family."

"Thank you, Mrs. Jackson."

"Your parents are on their way over. Don't look so alarmed. You two were going there next anyway, weren't you? So I thought it was time we all met. James!" Terri's mother called to her father. "Would you start the barbecue, darling? And how about mixing a nice pitcher of martinis?"

Nat's parents had three martinis apiece before Nat's father, Big Nat, punched his fist into his palm and stood up. "One thing I will not tolerate," he said, "is divorce." Six-foot-five and over three hundred pounds, he placed himself directly in front of Nat and Terri who sat side by side on a garden bench silently sipping their Cokes. He jabbed both index fingers at them. "You clowns," he began in a choked voice. "You clowns had better promise you will never divorce."

"Sit down," Nat's mother warned from the shadows. Mrs. Gunn worked for lawyers and still had her business suit on; she had hugged Terri's parents when she came in but she had not said a word to Nat or Terri all evening.

"Promise," Big Nat boomed. "Promise me you will not divorce."

"We promise," Nat and Terri said.

"I want to hear it."

"We *promise*."

"Okay then," Big Nat said, hands on hips, "so what's the plan?"

"We... we're..." Nat began.

"Speak up!"

"We're eloping to Reno tomorrow," Terri finished.

"You can't," Mrs. Gunn said.

Everyone turned to her.

"Nathaniel," Mrs. Gunn said, "is nineteen years old. Terri can marry anyone she wants but according to the law Nathaniel can't marry until he's twenty-one without our written permission."

"Even in Nevada?"

"Even in Nevada. So," Mrs. Gunn concluded, "we're going to Reno with them."

"Well if you're going," Terri's mother chimed in, "we're going too."

Terri's ten-year-old sister and eight-year-old brother, who had been staring at her stomach all night, began to hop up and down. "Can we come?" they asked.

"Of course," Terri's mother said. "It will be a party."

Terri turned to Nat for help but Nat was listening to her father. "You can drive the Porsche," her father was saying.

"With you, sir?" Nat stammered. "There's not room."

Her father sighed. "You can *drive* the Porsche."

"You're letting me drive the Porsche?"

"So I will go ahead and make reservations for all of us at The Mapes," Terri's mother decided. "Any preference for restaurants after the ceremony?" "Pizza," Terri's siblings chimed. "Kids?" Terri's mother said, turning to Terri and Nat.

"Nathaniel is allergic to seafood," Mrs. Gunn said.

"So we'll find someplace French. Or Italian." Terri's mother turned to the others, her voice bright. "Who's playing at Harrah's this weekend? Anyone know? God. I hope it's not Wayne Newton again."

"I like Wayne Newton," Big Nat said.

Terri threw up twice before leaving Saturday morning and she made Nat pull over once so she could throw up again by the side of the road. "Don't get any barf on the car," Nat said, worried. He had been driving at the precise speed limit ever since they'd left, his eye on the odometer, his foot hovering near the brake, too preoccupied to talk or even listen to the radio. Terri had been left with her own thoughts, which were mainly about her sour stomach, the three pounds she had already gained, and the clothes her mother had insisted on buying for her—a toffee-colored cocktail dress to get married in and a peignoir set with a padded bra for the wedding night. Both were hideous. As was the chiffon scarf holding Terri's hair back in the convertible, as was her hair itself, with its stiffly sprayed beauty shop chignon. Nat, as always, looked handsome, with his collar turned up, his sunglasses on, and his dark hair curled on his forehead. He was a good dresser, often changing his shirt twice a day; his nickname was Natty. He could answer every definition in the Word Power section of *The Readers' Digest*, played the bongos more or less on beat, could drive the length of Shattuck Avenue without hitting a red light and was famous for blowing smoke rings within smoke rings. Everyone liked him. Terri liked him. If only she loved him. She sighed, took the lit cigarette he handed her. They were stopping for lunch at a roadside restaurant with The Parents and then checking in to the hotel in Reno with The Parents and then going on to the chapel with The Parents and then going out to dinner with The Parents. "Glad someone's having fun," she murmured, exhaling.

"I cannot believe this baby," Nat said, but he was talking about the Porsche.

The Silver Bells Chapel had pink satin bows and sprays of white plastic lilies tied to the pews. The minister had a toupee and a thick southern accent. "Elmer Gantry," Terri whispered before she remembered that Nat hadn't seen that movie; she'd seen it with a red-haired Phi Delt; they'd kissed goodnight afterward; he'd said he'd call; he might be calling this minute. "Terri?" her roommate would say, picking up the phone in the upstairs hallway. "Oh, didn't you know? Terri got knocked up and had to leave school. But I'm free."

The waiting room they had been herded into was crowded but cheerful. "You look a little young to get hitched," a soldier in uniform said to Terri's brother who blinked shyly and didn't answer, though Terri's sister chimed in with a *"He's* not getting married, *she* is," pointing to Terri who wasn't sure but thought she might throw up again. Her new shoes pinched and there were fat half-moons of sweat already forming under the armpits of her too-tight dress. She caught her father's eye and looked away, furious. Standing in front of the mirror in her parents' hotel room, he had zipped her up an hour ago, saying, as he did, "You don't have to go through with this, you know," which is exactly what he should have said before, when she could have used it. She tightened her lips and tried to focus on the couple

191

who had just been called to the altar, two old people in Hawaiian shirts who had to be drunk to look so happy. "Next," her father said as their own names were called, and, not wanting to lift her elbow high enough for the sweat stains to show, Terri took his arm and they trotted briskly down the aisle.

Nat, looking young and unfamiliar in a new gray suit, was already waiting at the altar, his mother, stony-faced, beside him and his father weeping into a large white handkerchief. Nat flipped the tip of his tongue out between his teeth the cute way he did and fixed her with eyes so deep and liquid that for a second she could not stand it. He looked as if he really wanted to do this! Did he trust her that much? She wasn't trustworthy. All she wanted was to run out the door! But when he held his trembling hand out, Terri took it, glad for its warmth, glad for the first time that no one had thought to buy her a bouquet, as she wasn't sure how she would manage flowers and a ring too. "Left," Nat cued softly, as she reached to place the ring on the wrong hand, and then he giggled, and she giggled too, relieved, and then they kissed and then they were married.

They still could not drink, however. The Parents could, and did, growing louder with each toast during the interminable dinner. They had fallen in love with each other. "The best thing about Nat and Terri?" Big Nat kept slurring. "Jeanette and Robert!"

"Here, here," Terri's mother echoed, toasting Nat's parents in turn. Terri's brother and sister, ignored, poured salt and pepper all over the tablecloth, snuck under their chairs, fought with forks, stuck wine glasses into their coat pockets, raced in and out of the restrooms. Nat and Terri sat in silence, their knees pressed together under the table. "Don't look so stricken, you two," Terri's mother ordered gaily. "Marriage is fun."

"Saved my life," Big Nat agreed.

Mrs. Gunn, for the first time all day, looked at Terri. Terri knew Mrs. Gunn preferred Candy; she had seen Candy's photograph on her mantle. "Have you started to look for work yet?" Mrs. Gunn asked Terri now. "Because Nathaniel has to get his degree. That's part of the deal. Otherwise we won't support you."

"We can support ourselves."

"Shut up, Terri," Terri's father said grimly.

"Terri's got job interviews set up for next week," Nat offered.

"Where?" Terri's father turned, interested, eyebrows lifted.

"The bank," Terri lied, holding her breath, waiting for him to say, What bank? But her father said nothing and as she rose to go to the ladies' room she promised herself that she would, indeed, apply at every bank in the city. Also every department store, every insurance office. She left the table, her mother's words, "I was like that, had to pee every four minutes" ringing in her ears as she slipped through the restaurant and stood smoking outside the back door, looking out at the busy street with its glaring lights and crowds of total strangers. They were going to have to live with Nat's parents until they could afford their own apartment and the idea of sleeping in his bedroom with its cowboy wallpaper and towering sculptures of empty Marlboro boxes, of eating dinner with his parents every night and enduring their endless bridge games, made her sick. Nat had two more years of school. Then, when he got his degree in psychology, he would find a full-time job and she could go back to school herself. She missed school! Not the classes, exactly, though she'd give anything to be sitting in the auditorium again, listening to her history professor ramble on about the Punic Wars, but the green grassy Quad where she could lie under a tree and read Jane Austen all day, the café that served pecan pie with hard sauce, the red-haired Phi Delt she would never see again. She shivered in the warm air, wishing Nat would appear, take her elbow, and lead her away from here, just the two of them, on their own. But Nat was still at the table, obediently listening to her mother talk about her bladder. She stubbed her cigarette out and returned.

The bridal suite her parents had paid for was right next to her parents' bedroom and the loose headboard banged against the adjoining wall so forcibly that she and Nat ended up consummating their marriage on the floor that night, he still in his dress shirt, she tangled up in the peignoir set, which Nat actually seemed to like. It wasn't as nice as the first time they'd done it. Nat wouldn't let her muss his hair or touch his back and she hated having her neck sucked. "Goodnight, Mrs. Gunn," he said to her proudly before he fell asleep and Terri shivered, seeing his mother in her business suit, then lay awake remembering how she used to write that name out in Peacock Blue ink in the margins of her freshman notebooks, Mrs. Nathaniel Philip Gunn, Mrs. Theresa Anne Jackson Gunn. Was her mother right? Had she really wanted this? No! She had wanted Paris. She had wanted guitars in the moonlight and white horses and black coffees and intimate conversations that lasted all night. But she hadn't wanted any of it badly enough to work for it, had she. She hadn't, as her professors kept pointing out, applied herself. She rubbed a tear off her cheek and held her left hand up to study the new gold ring. Cheap. Ugly. But solid. Alarmingly solid.

Nat wasn't crying but he was blinking awfully fast as, an hour after leaving their families at a breakfast buffet in Reno and setting off to explore Lake Tahoe, they drove back to the gas station at the Cal-Neva border where he must have left the gas cap to the Porsche. It wasn't there. They asked the attendants, walked around and around the pumps—no gas cap. Nat plugged the tank with one of his sweat socks and they drove up and down the highway, scanning the asphalt in silence. Nothing Terri offered cheered him up. "Your father will never forgive me," was all he would say. Ignored and annoyed,

Underage

Terri pulled a Faulkner paperback out of her purse and read it as they drove, holding the pages down with her palm as the wind ruffled them. Late in the day, they parked by a hiking trail and trudged around the lake. They stopped at a lookout and did what honeymooners were supposed to do: looked out. Blue water, blue mountains, blue sky above. The air smelled like pine and potato chips and Sea 'n Ski. Nat turned her face toward his, tipped it up, and kissed her. Terri kissed him back. "It's going to be all right," she told him. But I'm not staying with you, she added to herself. This is just temporary. I will have the baby and then I will leave you.

And she might have left him, but something happened, something small, something obvious, something she should have picked up on long before. Nat got out of bed early that next morning and stood with his back to her, looking through the slats of their roadside motel room at the parking lot; maybe he hoped the gas cap had materialized in the night and magically reaffixed itself to the Porsche, or maybe, like her, he was simply thinking of a way to escape. His cowlick stood straight up, his shoulder blades jutted out, his buttocks were narrow as a child's, and a dusky dollop of testicle swayed between his thin thighs. He had never let her see him completely naked before, and his vulnerability touched her, but it was the condition of his skin that would keep her married to him for the next fifty-four years. Nat's entire backside was pitted and gouged with slashes of acne and dark purple boils. He might have been blasted by shrapnel, he might have been clawed by a tiger. He was deeply, horribly, secretly wounded. No one else knew it— not his friends, not his parents, not the doctors he refused to see—no one knew it but she. Shocked, repelled, disappointed, and, for the first time, deeply drawn to him, Terri closed her eyes. She did not mean to fall asleep but she did and when she woke up it was time to go home.

Hopeless

Scotty wasn't used to adults liking her, and Uncle Carl's good-natured wink scared her to death. Uncle Carl was her father's brother but he didn't look like any of the photographs of her father; he was fat and bald and had black hairs on the backs of his hands and a tattoo of a noose around his neck. Refusing to wink back, Scotty buckled herself into the seat of the pickup and stared straight ahead, hoping Uncle Carl wouldn't reach over and pinch her cheek, like he did once to Melissa, that time Melissa slapped him. "Ready to boogie?" Uncle Carl asked, flashing two gold teeth as he got in behind the wheel and turned the key. "Let's see if we can't set a record and beat the little duchess."

Scotty had no idea what boogie meant but she knew "the little duchess" referred to her cousin Melissa, who had talked their grandparents into buying her a plane ticket to Salt Lake City. Dov and Dada had phoned to tell Scotty how sorry they were they couldn't afford to fly her out as well. "I don't care," Scotty had lied. "I like to drive." Which she did, in a way; she was in no hurry to spend the summer at her grandparents' house and she liked looking out windows.

"Behave and remember to do everything you're told, Scotlyn," her mother called as Uncle Carl pulled out of the driveway. Uncle Carl honked and hollered, "She better not," which was simply incomprehensible, and then he gave Scotty another of those distressing winks before he reached for the radio and turned the game on, loud.

Scotty had no interest in baseball and she tuned out easily as she looked down at the book on her lap. She was the fastest reader in the Fifth Grade and knew she'd finish it before they got to Reno, which would leave her with nothing to do the rest of the trip. Usually she played Twenty Questions with Aunt Elcie but Aunt Elcie was staying home with the twins and having what her mother called "a nervous breakdown" because Uncle Carl had been out of work so long. The cab still smelled like the twins: talcum powder, sour milk, and throw up. Was there a forgotten diaper stowed somewhere? "You don't get carsick do you?" Uncle Carl asked as she straightened up from checking under the seat. "Smart girl like you?"

"I don't think intelligence has anything to do with kinetosis."

"Sure it does. Kine-what?"

Scotty adjusted her glasses and didn't answer.

Uncle Carl whistled. Then: "So what's your book about?"

"I haven't read it yet. So I don't know what it's about."

"Tell me anyway."

"It's part of a dragon cycle."

"That like a unicycle?"

Scotty was not going to answer that.

"Ever tell you I had a unicycle?"

Nor that. One of Uncle Carl's jobs had been in a carnival and he still did tricks. Scotty had seen him put the dollar bill in his ear at family picnics too often to still be impressed, though she never said No when, with a flourish, he pulled it out from his other ear and handed it to her.

"Yep. Rode it right down Main Street. Me and my pet bear."
She looked up.

"Yep," Uncle Carl nodded. "Blackie."

"Isn't that illegal?"

"Probably."

A bear. He would have to be caged. Maybe chained. He could be trained to dance and behave on walks. He would terrorize other people but not her. He would love her. Her voice cautious, Scotty asked, "What happened to him?"

"No idea; he's probably still around somewhere. Didn't your dad ever tell you about old Blackie?"

"I don't see my dad," Scotty reminded him. "He moved to Texas."

"That prick."

"Melissa said he's never coming back."

"Melissa, honey, I hate to say it, isn't a nice person."

Scotty didn't argue. It was true. If Melissa was here in the truck right now she would have her feet on the dash and her elbow in Scotty's throat. She would smell good though. Melissa always smelled good. She looked good too. She had grown three inches since she'd turned twelve, wore a bra, and swore in Mandarin. She would cover her ears and scream if she could hear Uncle Carl start to sing about a place called Crippled Creek with a chorus about a drunkard's dream which actually made Scotty a little nervous for she knew Uncle Carl used to have a problem that way though her mother said he'd made amends whatever that meant and had recovered.

"Your turn," Uncle Carl said. "I sing for you, you sing for me."

"I can't sing."

"Come on, Scotto, let's hear it. What's your favorite song? Belt it."

Scotty shook her head and slunk low in her seat. Her favorite song was, to her shame, "Let It Go" from *Frozen*, and no way was she going to sing that for Uncle Carl or anyone. Uncle Carl, surprising her, didn't insist, just shrugged and said, "Guess you'll have to listen to me the whole way then," and broke into something that sounded like an injured dog. All his songs sounded like dog songs—yipping, yapping, howling—and Scotty found it was as easy to tune them out as the ball game had been. She tugged at her new shorts, bought for this trip, and lifted her bottom to unstick herself from the vinyl seat. Her bare skin made a smacking sound she hoped Uncle Carl couldn't hear. She turned away to study the colorless landscape—strip malls, orchards, farmhouses set back from the road. She imagined a long sword extending directly from her window and cutting everything they passed in half: telephone poles, buildings, other cars, people.

"Of course your dad's coming back," Uncle Carl said suddenly. "What? You think he doesn't miss you every day?"

"I don't know."

"Well I do. You don't stop missing your little girl. Not ever."

"I've stopped missing him," Scotty said.

"Liar."

She didn't correct him. Her father was living with another woman who had another daughter of her own. End of story. Scotty was hungry and hoped they would stop for lunch soon, but when Uncle Carl explained he had to get to Nevada fast—there was a guy he'd promised to meet there—she unwrapped the sandwiches her mother had made and they ate the dry tuna fish and wilted lettuce as the truck chugged up into the mountains.

"Winnemucca," Uncle Carl promised. "How does a big fat bloody steak sound in Winnemucca?"

"Disgusting."

"You'll change your mind once you see it. You don't have to use the facilities yet do you?"

Scotty did but said no.

"We'll stop for gas soon," he promised.

They stopped for gas at the first stop over the Nevada border and when Scotty came out of the restrooms she saw Uncle Carl inside the convenience store playing a slot machine. "Try your luck?" he asked, handing her a quarter. "Just put a coin in and pull. It's easy."

Scotty did what he said and watched the tube with grapes and lemons spin until they stopped and yes, he was right, it was easy. And dumb. Uncle Carl handed her another coin but she shook her head and went back to the truck. She opened her book but must have fallen asleep in the sunshine for when she woke up the cab had darkened and they hadn't moved; Uncle Carl was still in front of the slot machines, only he was drinking a beer now, which was probably all right, her mother said one beer never hurt anyone. Still, they'd been here a long time. Melissa might have landed in Salt Lake by now. Did she dare honk the horn? She reached over and tapped it and Uncle Carl turned, slapped his forehead like a cartoon clown and came right out, beer bottle in one hand and a mound of silver in the other. "Here you go, schnooks," he said, reaching into his pockets and dumping what felt like a hundred heavy silver dollars into her lap. "Don't say I never did nothing for you."

"I won't."

"Good girl."

"I'll say you never did *anything* for me."

Again, the surprising laugh just when she was braced for a slap—her mother slapped—could she really get away with saying anything to this man? *No one likes a know-it-all*—she had heard that a hundred times. And it wasn't even true. If she knew it all, she wouldn't be the last one chosen in soccer every year, she wouldn't have to sit alone at lunch. Well, as the song said, let it go. Scotty plucked the coins, many of them stuck to her skin, off one by one, and poured a clanking stream of them into the glove compartment. Money was not something you threw away. Or dumped on people. Or plunked into rigged slot machines. No wonder Aunt Elcie was having a nervous breakdown.

She tugged at the hem of her shorts again as Uncle Carl sped out of the parking lot. "Who wears short shorts," Uncle Carl sang. He grinned, slapped her knee lightly, and whistled, "We wear short shorts."

Another stupid song and Scotty squinched away on the seat. She hated her legs, which were too thick, too pink, too hairy, and her uncle's voice was slurred and she hated that too. She turned her head aside, blinking back tears. What was she doing here anyway? She had campaigned hard to spend the summer at home, reading and watching TV while her mother was at work but her mother said that wasn't healthy so here she was, stuck in a smelly truck with her carnie uncle and once she got to Salt Lake it would be no better; Dov and Dada would make her go to church twice a week to pray for her runaway father and she would have to sleep on the sunporch with Melissa, who hated her. She brushed her cheek, turned to the window, and began to count the telephone poles and dead jackrabbits that littered the highway.

It was hot in Winnemucca and the casino behind the diner was half empty. Uncle Carl scouted the gaming tables and came back looking disappointed. "Guess I missed him," he said. "Just as well. We had a good run here five years ago. Times change." He settled into the booth heavily beside her and ate the pickle off her plate.

"Hey," she protested.

"You want it back?"

"No!"

"Here." He stuck his tongue out. Big fat gray tongue with a slime of green slashed across it.

"Ugh!"

"Take it, it's urine." He turned away from her as two men and an old woman came in and headed toward the casino in back. "Wait for me in the truck," he said.

It was too dark to read in the truck and Scotty waited a long time before Uncle Carl came out. He was silent as he clambered in and started the engine. "Got any money?" he asked, his voice pleasant. He smelled like smoke and sweat and something dark and sweet and oily.

"There's money in the glove compartment," she reminded him and when they next stopped for gas, somewhere in the middle of a vast dark nowhere, that is where he looked. Again he was gone a long time and again, trying not to be scared, she waited. She jumped when he rapped on the passenger door.

"Move over," he said, getting in her side and pushing her with his big hands toward the steering wheel. "You're driving."

"I can't drive!"

"Sure you can. Melissa drives all the time. Look. Here's the key, put it in, that's right, turn it to the right, good, you're a natural. Can you reach that pedal on the floor, stop saying you can't, Scotty, it's not true. Just stand up a little and stretch your leg down and do it. Got it? Good. Now hold on to the wheel, wait, I'll turn on the headlights, just hold 'er steady, that's right, see that white line? Keep it to your left, I'm just going to..." Uncle Carl said and toppled sideways, his huge head on Scotty's lap, pinning her behind the wheel as the truck began moving forward.

"I can't drive!" she screamed. She stared wildly into the dark. A huge rig of some sort, lights glaring, horn blaring, whooshed up from behind and passed with a loud hiss of wind. She felt a thump under the tires—another jackrabbit? She gasped when, accidentally turning the wheel, the truck turned as well. Were they still on the road? She could no longer see the white line; everything was dark. Yet the engine continued to throb beneath her thighs and the wheel tingled under her grip. She turned the wheel one way, then another. Were they going in circles? This was like riding an animal—a bear, an eagle, some creature heavy and swift but obedient—trainable! Melissa always said Scotty couldn't cross a room without falling on her face. Her mother wouldn't let her dry knives. Her father, that prick, took the tennis racket from her hand one day and hit her over the head with it. Hopeless, he'd said. Yet here she was with Uncle Carl who might be dead driving a pickup truck straight through the desert. By herself! She leaned forward, pressed her foot to the pedal and heard her own voice, weirdly on key, rise up to sing words of her favorite song.

My X

My X never finishes his sentences. He'll start off with a "Did you see..." and then stop. When we first met, I thought it was charming. I'd prompt him. "Did I see what, darling?" Silence. After we were married, less charmed, I'd jump in with my own offerings: "Did I see the full moon last night, did I see the red dog, did I see the fat man in drag?" I was never right. My X would listen, correct me, and disappear. He could, literally, disappear, an act that should have made us money. "I think I'll go..." he'd say, and I'd chip in with a hopeful, "...to the store?" only to hear him say "...to India." One minute he'd be standing next to me and the next minute he'd be in a cab heading out to some seaport or in bed asleep or in the garden watering the roses he claimed I never took care of. At the end, in the lawyers' office, when I admitted that I never knew where he went, what he did, or whom he did it with, he shook his head sadly and said that was because I could not read his mind. "She's so..." he said to the lawyer.

"...exhausted," the lawyer and I said together.

"...impatient," he said.

It was true. And why not. Years had passed and I still didn't know him. In fact, that was what he often said to me: *You'll never know how much I love you* he'd say, and then, not unkindly, he'd laugh.

After the divorce there were sightings. A friend saw him in an art museum trying on silk scarves. My sister saw him pass her on the bridge in a silver Jaguar. A neighbor heard him talking Farsi with an Iranian rug dealer. We decided he either worked for the CIA or the FBI or the DEA or all three of them. Just last week, five years after our divorce, I bumped into him in a bookstore; he was standing in a corner reading the obituaries in *The New York Times* out loud to himself. He was dressed in surfer shorts and a hoodie. He had grown a mustache and had a pair of mirrored sunglasses on.

"Hi," I said.

He looked up, unsurprised. "Oh hi," he answered. "How are..."

"I'm fine," I said.

"...the roses?"

I took a deep breath. He looked thin and raggedy. It occurred to me he might be homeless.

"I'm having the Witherspoons over for lunch on Sunday," I said. "Our old neighbors. Would you like to come?"

"Do they still have their two..."

"Poodles? Yes."

"...timing son-in-law living with them?"

"Lunch is at noon," I said. "And I never slept with their son-in-law if that's what you're thinking."

"How do you know..."

"What you're thinking?"

"...whether he's still living with them or not."

"Noon," I repeated.

I was shaking when I left.

Sunday came and of course no X. The Witherspoons and I had barbecue and gin and tonics and had just settled into the living room to watch the U.S. Open when the poodles started barking and the son-in-law said, "There's a man in your back yard." I shrugged his hand off my thigh and stood up. My X was in the garden watering the roses. It was as if no time had passed. I went out to him.

"Did you see…" he said.

"No," I said. "I didn't. Hand me that hose please."

He handed me the hose and I aimed the nozzle straight at him and the blast was so strong it knocked him butt-down and his fake mustache flew off. For a second I exulted. Then because I'm an idiot I dropped the hose and went to help him up but he tripped me and I fell down hard beside him as the water spiraled fast and cold over both of us. He wrapped his arms around me and rocked us back and forth on the grass, laughing, and I felt his old male strength and smelled his sour green apple smell and for a second I was almost happy again. By the time I pushed him off and shook myself and stood, of course, nothing was left but a trail of damp footsteps in the grass, a thread from his hoodie snagged on the gate, tire marks on the curb. I ran out to the street as his bike rounded the corner, took my shoe off, threw it, missed. The last thing I heard was his voice, faint on the wind. "Don't worry dear, it's not…"

"Funny," I shouted.

"Over," he said, and disappeared.

The Author

MOLLY GILES is the award-winning author of six story collections and one novel. Most notably, *Rough Translations* won The Flannery O'Connor Prize, the Boston Globe Award, and The Bay Area Book Reviewers' Award; *Creek Walk* won The Small Press Best Fiction Award, the California Commonwealth Silver Medal for Fiction, and was a New York Times Notable Book; *Bothered* won the Split Oak Press Flash Fiction Award; and *All The Wrong Places* won the Spokane Prize for Fiction. Her work has also earned The O. Henry Award and the Pushcart Prize, and she has received grants from the National Endowment for the Arts, the Marin Arts Council, and the Arkansas Arts Council.

With thanks to the following journals that have previously published some of these stories.

Bellevue Literary Journal
Chicago Quarterly Review
Cimarron Review
CNET
COG
Fiction International
Fiction South East
Foliate Oak
Juked
Louisville Review
Missouri Review
Narrative
New Flash Fiction Review
Newport Review
Rattapallax
Smokelong Quarterly
Southern Review
Story/Houston
Superstition Review
The Midnight Oil
The Pinch
Two Sisters Writing
Ursa Minor
West Marin Review
Wigleaf
Willow Springs
Word Riot
Zyzzyva